DISSONANCE

DISSONANCE

The Furry Files

ADAM T. APPLEBAUM

Adam Thomas Applebaum - The Forsaken Scribe

This is a work of fiction. Names, characters, places, and incidents are either a product of the author's imagination or are used fictitiously. Any resemblance to actual people, living or dead, events, or locales is entirely coincidental. Opinions or actions in this novel do not reflect the author's existing viewpoints. They should not be taken as threats, political affiliations, or disrespect to anyone or any people who may feel portrayed in this novel.

First Edition: May 17, 2023

ISBN-13: 978-0-9970505-3-0
Library of Congress: 20239044244

Published by Adam Thomas Applebaum - The Forsaken Scribe
www.theforsakenscribe.com

The Following book is dedicated to Lynn Cantu. She provided all the funding for creating this book, and I am thankful for that. I hope it is to her liking. Moreover, I hope it is good with the readers as well. I also wish to mention that all events within this book are fictitious. Any names authentic or suspiciously similar to actual people, businesses, or other entities are coincidental. They should not be seen as an attack on anyone or an attempt to defame them. I also have the utmost respect for all agencies and entities that defend the country so we can have the luxury of worrying about things other than getting killed by terrorists or other bad actors in the world or people who once served such roles. Actions portrayed here are intended to be seen as isolated from my opinions. Any lack of realism is intended to make the book enjoyable and is best consumed with a suspension of disbelief. Thank you for reading

CONTENTS

ACKNOWLEDGEMENTS

This book was brought to you by Lynn Cantu, for she paid me to make it for her. Thanks also to MyJewishLearning.com for the Hebrew text used in this novel's prayer for repentance puzzle. Even though I could have pulled it as the public domain from nearly any source, theirs was the easiest to access and inclusion for this novel. I also wish to thank Sonia Dickson and Robin Shipley for helping me find employment that sustained me so I would not need to crowd-fund money to keep myself alive while paying rent and working on this novel. Thank you also to my parents for birthing me, raising me, and putting up with me all these years despite everything I put them through.

Thank you to my siblings for taking it in stride, as fictional depictions and allegories to them have to this day, been less than flattering but necessary for the plots I put together. I abstain from mentioning them by their actual names to protect them. On that note, thank you also to Nathaniel Cole and your girlfriend Danni for taking their representations in stride and supporting my earlier works with your purchases of them. Apologies to Nathaniel about the second poem from Into the Mind Out to Nature. Were it not bad enough I showed you in front of your mate once that I wrote it when I had got the wrong idea of who you were, I realize in retrospect going the extra mile to self-publish it as one of 25 poems from that book was a dick move. Though it remains in my collection, I see it now more as a testament to how easy it can be to get the wrong idea about someone when they grow up sheltered as I was from how things are in the real world. I admit my mistake and hope it can be taken as a work of satire instead of expressing any bitterness now.

Thank you to my roommate Nicole Sanders in particular, who had to hear my incessant click-clacking these late nights of my keyboard and my less-than-organized ways at times since I moved in September 2022. I am improving in this area in no small part by the urging of my caring ally Emily Grace Fine a KJ at Executive Suite that makes entertaining commentary and keeps me on my paw tips in the best of ways. Through her encouragement, I am taking steps to improve the functionality of what I have as well as storing away that which would be an eyesore. Thank you to Leonard Sinatra for allowing me to show off and do unofficial book signings within their place of Business.

CHAPTER 1

PRESCHOOL AND PREJUDICE

Hate Rises from the Rubble!

Torrance is a lovely town. We have our Old Town charm of decades gone by, a beach, and a shopping mall that was once the largest in America until Mall of America came around, or so people tell me. My name is Laila Yarakah. I am a female anthropomorphic silver-blue fox, and I have lived on Earth since 1947 and have been alive even longer. If one were to guess, I'd hardly look a day over 25. Some may recall the Civil Rights Movement of the 1960s. Well, safe to say, it seemed like as good of a time as any for us to come out in support. And we did. We were taken away and sent to Area 51 until someone publicly leaked our capture information for the entire globe to see. The human race was much less hesitant to accept their variations of each other when far different creatures existed. While we ultimately came to earn our freedom under immense public pressure from activists who sympathized with what it was to be different, that did not entirely make us comrades in arms. Though granted equal rights, there have been tensions between the human race and the various furry races of the world in light of these mutant chimpanzees' less-than-utopian tendencies. Sorry, the Intergalactically correct word is "intelligent life." Yeah, the United Planets phoned that one in. Live with them as long as I do, and you'll find it is highly inaccurate on average. Yes, they can speak as we do, and our communicators help with any mistranslations, but that does not mean they are talented at much. There are exceptions, of course, but even the smartest have their oafish moments.

I was a nurse at Harbor City Hospital, caring for adults and children, respectively. I would often keep plush toys in the trunk and sometimes backseat of my car out of habit. It was a comfort to them as much as a delight to me to see their smiling faces when they brave intensive care procedures with the help of a plush toy. While there, I met a cat boy with two striped tails and black and white fur far as the eye could see, with a few red highlights before the tips of his tails and in certain other equivalent places. His name was Adam, and from what he told me before the incident at the hospital, he could hardly fit in living in Covina. No surprise being the only furry family there, it took some getting used to for the conservative masses that called it home. Furries, as a rule, tend to lean more liberally, with some exceptions on most issues.

Jane, the receptionist, greeted him, "Aww, what a cutie is he in need of a doctor?"

Joanne shook her head, "No. On the contrary, he wishes to volunteer here to get a feel for the life of a doctor."

"Very well, just fill out the following forms, and we'll have him cheering up patients in no time."

After some tedious paperwork, Adam was led to the back room.

"Bye, Adam. See you when you get home."

Adam was walking by when he spotted me. I waved to him as the receptionist explained the situation and handed him over to me.

"Ah, just in time.

"We have a few patients for you to visit.

"By the way, you look kind of familiar..."

"Oh, you might know my dad, David. He is a Health Physicist in the research section of this place.

"He says he sometimes comes around to help measure the radiation levels of patients here since some doctors are afraid of handling radioactive materials."

"Ah, so you are his son.

"No wonder you looked so familiar.

"I know you will grow up to do amazing things one day."

Adam let out a cute meow and went to a few rooms. In one, he found a pretty girl recovering from surgery to fix a broken bone. He sat near her as she petted him.

Just then, her older brother came by to check up on her. "Hey, cat, beat it!"

"Leave him alone, Leon. He is just a volunteer."

"Stay out of this, Laura. His kind aren't nothing but trouble!"

Adam was frozen with fear. Leon closed in and threw a punch, but I quickly grabbed Adam out of the way. Leon hit the wall with his bare fist and became a temporary patient. Security took him to another room until then to ensure the safety of the volunteer cat boy.

"Thank you for stepping in.

"I suppose I should tell you how I got here like this.

"As you might imagine, it is hard not to be the center of attention living in Covina as the only cat family on the block.

"My mom drove me here and encouraged me to volunteer since I had expressed a childhood interest in being a doctor.

"I figured it beat the awkwardness of being petted by children when I just want to go to the library and read books.

"Books that are a bit more advanced than the feel-good ones usually recommended to kids my age.

"Though I did pick up a book about a teen who had run away from home and managed to carve out a home and rough it in the wilderness for years before his family joined him.

"I was reading it intently when suddenly I was surrounded by children who petted me and exclaimed about me being a kitty person.

"The parents, of course, apologized, and I told them I did not know what to make of this as I had never been petted before but was not particularly angry.

"I checked out the book and went home and heard about this position, so I thought, 'Why not?'

"If people are so intent on petting me, I may as well lend myself to people who need companionship."

"That makes sense.

"Boy, what a vivid story for one so young.

"You ever thought of writing a book about this?"

"Maybe one day, but I am doubtful anyone would want to read it."

"You never know, all sorts of people publish memoirs and autobiographies and find satisfaction in it even if they do not become world famous."

"Time will tell, but there are many more patients to cheer up, so I will get back to it."

With that, things mainly returned to routine. I would change bedpans and give out plush toys to kid patients when I could. I noticed he carried around a distinct glow-in-the-dark teddy bear that he got from his grandmother. I did a bit of curious digging, found out where they were made, and added some to my collection of toys I give to patients and the deserving.

My Career changed when a man named Bill Benson approached me with a business card and told me that I could work on something significant for the world and help change it in even greater ways than I could as a hospital nurse. I would have only likely gone into Hospice care from there if I earned my stripes, so I put in my paperwork as one did when switching jobs and went along with it once I verified the job was legit.

Wednesday, December 14, 1994, I started my job as a forensic anthropologist after completing my intensive training. For the first case, they sure gave me a hard one. A preschool in Covina burned to the ground, and nothing can be found, not even a bone. Depending on traffic, Covina is between an hour and a half to two hours by car. That's when the beach backdrop turned to a fast-food drive-thru called Dog Fart Burger for respecting intellectual property.

"Hello, welcome to Dog Fart Burger!

"Would you like to try the Two Pattie Barbeque Dog Fart Burger Combo?"

Those words came out of the digital confessional box repurposed to serve the public some food on the fly.

"No, thank you, I will have the Atomic Chicken Fart Sandwich combination with Easter Island Fries and a Large Meow Beer to drink."

"Would you like to try a Gee Whiz Cake with that?"

"Sure, why not."

I drove up to the window where a man who looked like he had too much caffeine stood ready to take my money and give me my food.

"Hello, that will be $4.00, please."

The cash exchange happened, and I pulled into a parking spot. Inside was a mix of humans and Furries chowing down at separate tables. Though they were in the same restaurant, one side seemed like furry creatures and the other humans. As for me, I sure would have found it convenient to have a pair of prehensile tails at a time like this; then again, one shouldn't drink and drive, nor should one eat while on the road. I pondered this amid my decidedly questionable dietary choice in my primitive compact car equipped with a Middle Finger Escape Rocket feature just in case things get too hairy. Only privileged people can access these vehicles lest they fall into the wrong hands.

A lunch that was as grubby inside as outside devoured, and tasted like spicy chicken and waffles. No doubt they had just finished serving breakfast and could not wash the taste of the battered breakfast out of the fry baskets. The road was to be my friend for the next couple of hours. Light traffic the whole way, the freeway never felt so free. It was short-lived, and the 1950s-looking town surrounded me like all good things in what felt like a blink. And come to find the vacant lot that was once the Covina Preschool was there.

Out of the car, the PI Patrick Paterson turned to me. "This is a case for the ages, to put it lightly.

"Nothing but ashes.

"We collected some for analysis at the lab, but we thought you'd want to see it yourself."

"And what of the suspects and survivors?"

"There is a two-tailed cat boy who remembers what went on that day despite allegedly leaving for the day.

"He said it was a dream or premonition.

"Surprised a kid his age knows what that is."

"Surprised you found your way out of a box when you were a kid."

"Touché."

With the witty banter out of the way, it was time to get to work. Every inch was searched for anything the PI may have missed.

Ashes to Ashes, dust to dust, could there be more, or have my analytical skills been left to rust?

That's it! Rust... plumbing is an essential requirement of any preschool.

"PI, have you any floor plans of the place or anything to suggest the layout it once had?"

"Yes, we do."

With the plans in hand, it appeared that the bathroom was nowhere to be found, but definite signs of formerly intact water lines.

"Well, that rules out cherry bombs.

"Whatever did this must have had some high-level clearance to make this mess."

"Indeed, the detective interrogated a cat boy, but he kept saying something was wrong with the ornaments he set up when the supervisor sent him home."

"And you all took it as a confession?"

"Nah, no judge would ever believe he could have purposely tampered with anything and left so little evidence.

"Whoever it is, they probably know what gives it away and have studied crime fiction passionately.

"That or someone on the inside, but who do we know that would hate children this much?"

"Beats me, but supposing it was a structural failure, it could be a class action negligence suit.

"The floor plans look like they were built for housing before earthquake standards."

I dusted for prints, hoping to find anything to close this case. I didn't find anything at first, but then I tripped over a skull as I turned around to consider alternate tactics.

"Are you okay, Laila?"

"Yes, I am fine, Patrick.

"Woah, how did we not discover this before?"

"Don't know, but it sure seems odd cause I swear we checked all over and found nothing until now.

"For all we know, the preschool could have been built on an ancient burial site."

"Regardless, I will want to take these remnants back to the lab to make sure."

After digging up more fossils than a museum could ever hold and other evidence, life was once there; it was back to the lab for me if there was one; our perp was either a criminal mastermind who had buried these as decoys to hide his crime or careless, thinking we would never find out. After running the analytics, we identified the bodies of several parents and children. From the looks of things, they had a whole house for the event. It was not a surprise when it was free entry as a thank you for enrolling the children. Lily Lockup's daughter, Lauren Lockup, and her husband, Loman Lockup, were among the victims. Nothing conclusively linked Adam to the tragedy for as many bodies as we had identified. In the end, it seemed like the cause of the building burning and collapsing was nothing more than a combination of faulty electrical wiring and unstable ornaments that ignored fire codes put in place to protect people. Naturally, since the two-tailed cat boy had presumably seen the event happen before it did, many people seemed to shun him by association.

Not long after the report, the defunct Hammer and Tail Construction Company members and even the former Mayor of Covina,

Monty Moneybags, were tried for criminal negligence in the preschool building. The plans had suggested that whatever caused the preschool's destruction was at least partly the fault of it not being up to building standard from the beginning. It took a while to get the case going, both for finding an impartial jury and a Defense and Prosecuting attorney who did not lose loved ones in the tragedy. At the same time, a case was being built with the evidence I had found. Legal experts know this as the discovery portion; I opted to stay in Covina for a while at a Holiday Inn. It was the one by the West Covina Freeway. Call it a sixth sense, but somehow, I knew trouble was brewing, and tomorrow was my day off. According to news reports, the incident with the preschool could not have come at a worse time, as Mr. Moneybags had just lost the Governor's Election that year and was planning a campaign for the next one. I turned the TV to channel 12 GN for Generic News, and this was what I saw.

"Good evening, everyone.

"My name is George Generic of Generic News, and tonight's top story Mayor Moneybags, an unsuccessful contender in the last California Gubernatorial race, is facing immense controversy.

"It involves a pending class action lawsuit and criminal negligence suit over a poorly made structure he commissioned while Mayor of Covina.

"Meanwhile, Senator Silverstein took office earlier this month after he created a winning campaign against Former Mayor Moneybags on kissing adorable San Joaquin kit foxes.

"In other news, despite the cause of the destruction of Covina Preschool being attributed to it not being up to safety codes in multiple categories, residents of Covina are not convinced.

"We now go live to GN Reporter Terry Tellme."

"Thank you, George; I am here at the house of a two-tailed cat named Adam.

"As you can see, swastikas are mowed into his family's lawn, and someone has spray painted the words 'a predator lives here, protect your children' on his garage door.

"Behind me are some protesters as well.

"Let's talk to one of them."

"Yeah, the name is Gil Go-Away, and I have lived in this fine town for too long to think something wasn't up."

"Why might that be?"

"Think about it, he is a cat, and they are a predatory species

"On top of that, the team sent to investigate was a group consisting of at least half Furries and of a known pro-furry organization hired by the police force.

"You don't see where there might be a conflict of interest?"

"No more than having a jury of your peers determine guilt."

"Well, he should make like my last name and go away."

"And now we turn to the cat boy."

Just then, Adam came out to talk and was seen being pelted with eggs and rotten banana peels.

Adam shook it off, "Besides the vandalism and being pelted with trash, I cannot even get an ice cream without people whispering things about me, refused service at eateries, and even threats from parents, not the least of which is Lily Lockup.

"Thankfully, the legal system knew better than to let her play any part in the upcoming court cases.

"I fear what might transpire if others like me are mistreated this way."

"And there you have it, and what a brave boy to endure this."

With that TV, time was over. How awful that anyone, least of all a child, is subject to such harassment. There has to be something we can do until this all blows over.

There was a knock on my hotel door. How strange why would anyone be coming to call at this hour? My thoughts were promptly answered when I looked through the peephole to see what else but the cat who was attacked today.

"Sorry to disturb you, but... the police are searching my house for clues. Because I had an idea what became of the preschool and the public pressure, they need to check again."

"But they already ruled out that it couldn't be you."

"That or they are searching for clues to the vandals who made a mess of my home.

"The public did not trust your team's work on this case.

"I could end up on trial soon if they find anything suspicious, and I am scared."

"I am sorry you saw this side of the world so soon.

"I had hoped you'd at least be in high school before you saw this kind of prejudice.

"If it is any relief, I am sure they are probably looking into the vandalism and whether or not someone could have faked evidence pointing in your direction.

"If it is that, they could use the evidence to find the vandal and make them pay to get your property fixed."

"I don't think it would make that big a difference.

"I am tired of living in a place where I am unwanted.

"If they push me too far, I might lose control of myself and become the monster they fear I am."

"You're not a monster.

"It is they that are the real monsters."

"I wish it were that simple."

This is no good.

I cannot, as a professional, give in to emotions or compassion.

Though he may be cute, I have to remember anyone can be a criminal in this place.

But how in the world would he possibly be behind something like this, and how could people give into such heresy even though any educated person would see the folly in assuming he could do it without help?

Before I could think another thought, the scared cat boy hugged my legs and purred.

Well, there goes any lack of bias I might have had for him.

Regardless, I'm sure I could testify appropriately about who did this.

"Well, where are your parents, little one?"

"They are staying at Pie Tights next door near the freeway leading out of town."

"Pie tights?"

"Adam pulls out a photo of the sign that looks like a royal crown with the words 'Excellent' and 'Cowboy Movie' on it."

"Oh, that place."

"Yeah..."

"Curious. Why do you call it that?"

"Not entirely sure, but my mom says I have been calling it that since I was 2 or 3 years old."

"I also mistook the Crypt Keeper as a monkey for the way he laughed when I was about that age too."

"Well, if you look at it that way, it looks like a meringue pie.

"And I imagine we have earthquakes here; they had to screw it in tight."

"And the Crypt Keeper, well yeah, he does have a pretty weird inhuman laugh."

"Makes as much sense to me as anything else."

"It is cute.

"Don't ever forsake your childhood no matter what may befall you.

"Moreover, how did you find me here?"

"There aren't very many of us living in this town, so all I had to do was wander the area until I picked up the scent that wasn't human, and I followed it here."

"Your parents must be worried if they're in that hotel room.

"I would return if I was you."

"Alright..."

With that, the tragic cat boy let me be. I'd probably take him in as my own if he were an orphan. Then again, my line of work would be too dangerous to have a child. Though I am not a police officer, I'd be a fool to think that a place this hostile to him on the mere suspicion of his involvement wouldn't have it out for me, too, due to my work on it.

Once I was alone, I deadbolted my motel door and went to sleep for the night. In the morning, I would explore the place further.

The following day came, and after I completed my morning routine and stepped outside, I found everything was mainly calm, contrary to what I'd seen on tv the day prior, but I knew better than to let my guard down. Call it personal interest, but I had to know if the investigators found anything at the cat boy's house. When I arrived, I found the team sent to investigate was just about to give up and was tearing down the police tape.

"Wait!"

"What, who are you?"

"I'm Lailah Yarakah.

"I am a new forensic anthropologist."

"Well, no one got killed here, so I don't think we need you on this part of the case.

"We didn't find a motive for the cat boy in your case either."

"I wasn't suggesting that, but of the people who lost loved ones.

"Did any of them set off red flags that would suggest they'd have done this to spite him?"

"Not really.

"If anything, this looks like the sort of thing some high school delinquents would do even if he weren't a crime suspect."

"I see. Thank you for your time."

I wandered away from the scene. I don't know what I expected to learn from this crime scene that wasn't on the news, but something told me there was something much bigger than it seemed, and I couldn't place it. Either way, when they finally got the hearing, I was sure I'd be called an expert witness to give my side of things, so I had to make sure my theory was straight. Finding nothing else of interest, I checked out of the hotel around the same time as Adam and his family. We waved goodbye to each other while his parents seemed confused about how he might know me. I headed on the road back to Torrance.

Once home, it would be business as usual until the court dates. On January 07, 1995, the mail came. I was to appear in West Covina Courthouse on February 01, 1995, and to bring documents about my findings and expert opinion based on all I could uncover. For those who do not know, such a subpoena requires 25 days advance notice if served by mail. Based on the date stamp when I opened it, it had been mailed on January 04, 1995. More than enough time for such an instate sending to arrive within the required time. Adam had also received one as well. The civil class action suit would happen on March 01, 1995. Still, I would not need to be there in civil cases, despite the criminal ones being related. Civil cases do not use character witnesses and can use evidence such as floor plans I found a while back and the reasonable person's clause to determine damages to all parties involved. Since the cases applied to both Monty Moneybags and the members of the defunct Hammer and Tail construction company on the same facts, it was determined more efficiently by the appropriate judges that both criminal and civil cases were joint ones.

Inside the courtroom, Judge Accurate took his seat.

"Alright, we will now hear the case of Hammer and Tails Construction Company and Monty Moneybags VS Covina."

Both parties were sworn in, and the judge would hear the opening statements starting with the prosecuting attorney Sara Stockade.

"Your honor, the recent tragedy at what was supposed to be a festive occasion is nothing short of appalling.

"The evidence we have to present will show that these horrible people are guilty of criminal negligence, involuntary manslaughter, and third-degree murder."

Defense Attorney Simon South Sea said, "And I intend to show the evidence is insufficient to declare them guilty of anything short of maybe civil penalties, if that."

Judge Accurate nodded and let them proceed.

"Exhibit A is the DNA sample from the bones found at the site of the tragedy.

"Exhibit B is the floor plans for the construction that both Moneybags and the multiple members of the Hammer and Tails construction company signed.

"Lastly, Exhibit C is the written statement from the expert in the field who I have brought into court to answer questions about the situation."

"And I have a witness that was there the day the incident happened.

"He was setting up for the play that went afoul, and his story indicates that something was wrong with the play setup and not the building itself."

Judge Accurate first examined the physical evidence brought to him in discovery and spoke.

"So, according to what I see here, the photos accompanying the DNA samples were people on the collapse site?

"The floor plans and statement suggest that corners were cut in securing the building for earthquake resistance.

"Moreover, highly flammable materials were inside the building beyond what is typical for a place of early childhood education."

"Yes, in the plans are substandard switchboards and timber wood, which would require maintenance to prevent rotting.

"Were a switchboard to be faulty, it poses an electrical fire which could burn the timber wood and result in a building collapse."

"Your honor, even if we accept that the building wasn't made with the best of materials because, let's face it, cities aren't corporations and have too many priorities to account for everything, it still doesn't explain the circumstances surrounding the collapse itself.

"I'd like to call Adam Apfelbaum to the stand to explain how he remembers it happening."

Adam nervously took the stand, and the judge turned to him.

"Mr. Apfelbaum, please explain what you remember of the day you helped set up the play."

"Yes, your honor. It was a day like any other, except we were preparing to put together a show for the parents.

"As we were setting it up, I noticed that the concert lights were shaking a bit despite the fact the person ensuring I did the job safely saw it as nothing to worry about.

"Moreover, they had me set up an angel that would fly as we sang silent night around the room.

"The show was supposed to be a musical complete with a nativity scene.

"I was just to be a stagehand because I didn't want to be a part of the show, but participation in some features was mandatory for all children.

"I expressed my concerns that maybe having a flying angel bust be carried across the room on wires when we could barely get the lighting to stay put was not a good idea, but they didn't listen.

"While I admit I wasn't there to see exactly how it went down, I suspected something was up between the barely hanging lights, ambitious, moving props, and the cracks in the ceiling as I attempted to hang the rope that would carry it across."

Defense Attorney Simon South Sea looked proud as he prepared to give his interpretation of those facts.

"So, these were maintenance and show-related problems, not that of a faulty building.

"I mean, they had freaking kids setting up props, and they didn't think maybe they should reinforce that stuff?"

"Objection! The age of the volunteers setting up decorations is irrelevant here.

"They were supervised by people who should have safety standards.

"As we cannot interview the dead, we cannot know if the people using the building knew of its defects, which is the crucial component of the negligence case.

"If there is nothing further, I call my expert to the stand Laila Yarakah."

I took the stand calmly, "It would seem some of the things I wrote in my report, among other bits of evidence, may not have been as clear as I had hoped.

"The bones we found at the site from which we took DNA were not initially discovered until I arrived.

"Based on what Adam said on the stand and relevant spec documentation from my report, it sounds like the adults thought it was okay that things were moving a little as they put it up.

"Thus, it was likely a known defect of the building itself.

"While this may be normal with hanging ornaments, light fixtures moving should have been a major red flag.

"There were also cracks in the ceiling which is usually one of the telltale signs something is wrong with a building on an inspection report.

"That would be consistent with the lack of earthquake reinforcement and possible rot suggested earlier.

"A responsible construction company would have warned the person who asked the building to be built about it and billed it accordingly so the rot wouldn't happen, and it would be the burden of the current owners to keep it maintained.

"At no point in the public records of the defunct company in question was there ever a bill for such a thing.

"Not in this building or the others they had worked on.

"Based on the billing statements, they used cheap materials that were barely pliable and should have been disposed of.

"They didn't, and how they managed to keep it standing this long is miraculous.

"Based on what was found and the history of the building on public records, it would seem that even if they didn't hang décor from the ceiling as described, that building would have collapsed under itself sooner or later.

"Given there wasn't much left of the rubble, it was likely an electrical fire."

Judge Accurate turned to the Defense Attorney, "So from what I gather, there were defects in the building demonstrated through evidence, record, and examination of what was left of the preschool.

"Therefore, the Hammer and Tails construction company knowingly used parts that were not up to standard and would eventually collapse regardless of provocation by whoever used them."

"Um, your honor I..."

"Save it... no matter who was unjust to who, both of your defendants knew what they were getting into, and because all parties were too cheap to get a proper construction, hundreds of people died almost two months ago.

"Were this a situation involving weapons that you used to harm intentionally, this would be apparent first-degree murder. At best, it is third-degree murder, criminal negligence, and manslaughter.

"As the event did not count ticket sales, my best judgment metric is the number of enrolled people who could not be found. The enrollment led to conservatively 100 counts of manslaughter, 100 counts of third-degree murder, and a count of criminal negligence for each of your parts in what ensued.

"The mayor at the time was paying these people to do what they did, and despite a city inspector warning them about the building, they approved it anyway.

"Therefore, they are just as guilty as those who left it this way.

"The ones who left it this way could have made the necessary adjustments, billed him anyway, and sued in civil court for what needed to be done, but they did not, as their business history shows.

"Has the Jury reached a verdict?"

The Jury Responded, "Guilty as charged."

Judge Accurate said, "I sentence all defendants to no less than 25 years in jail.

"We are adjourned now; take this scum away."

Everyone went home after that except the ones sentenced to jail time.

CHAPTER 2

REVENGE IS BITTERSWEET

When Sorry Won't Cut It!

The next day was business as usual for me. Thanks to the evidence, my team and I found the defunct company called Hammer and Tails Construction's members. Monty Moneybags and Hammer and Tails Members were sentenced to a minimum of 25 years for Third Degree Murder, criminal negligence, and involuntary manslaughter. This a pretty light sentence considering how many children and parents died in the tragedy, but to be fair, it did not seem like any of them wanted this to happen, and they just were too cheap to put it together safely. But it did not matter. Senator Silverstein had already won the election before the case even happened. Good thing, too, because although he is human, he is pro-furry.

My next job took me to San Diego. That is not unusual if you know that our organization is not directly affiliated with any specific Police Precinct but instead, an agency for hire that just happened to get called in for cases throughout California. It seems an odd detail to mention here, but it seemed relevant since, up to this point, we mainly had worked on criminal cases within Los Angeles County, so this would be our first case since I was hired that went outside county lines. Essentially, we are like contractors for criminal investigations and have a mixed bag for clients. Nevertheless, that only gave us the license to help police with some of the more complex cases and by no means gave us status as officers of any rank. That did not stop people from giving us inside intel on some instances of interest, though, especially if they thought they might need our help. Despite this, since we were hired by law enforcement for most of our cases, we adopted the name "Furry Investigation Department 310" for ourselves when addressing us as a group based on our primary focus and the area code of where we were based.

Our company decided only one such team could be based in each area code. The rule was to avoid confusion as far as it pertained to our company. If another chapter of our firm sprung up in Covina, it would be called Furry Investigation Department 626 or 818, depending on the city's area code. If it used multiple area codes, we would use the one consistent with the neighborhood area code where our building was based. We are, however, sent out to different jurisdictions afforded to us based on our performance, skill set, and other circumstances surrounding the case. Other investigation agencies not affiliated with us could otherwise establish themselves in the same city. The long and the short of it is, putting a dream team like us together was not easy, but we took advantage of the fact we were not police despite them being our top clients to allow us to go anywhere we needed to be.

When I left my home, I spotted a familiar-looking fast-food worker heading to work on foot. Unless my work stress got to me, I swear he is the same one who took my order. Maybe it is just the caffeine many of us depend on to get through the mundane, but there was something subtly unsettling about him that I could not place. He seemed to know things he was eager to tell people, but no one wanted to hear them. Is he following me? No, that cannot be right. Get it together, Laila; he is just a happy cashier. He could not be behind, much less privileged to anything this huge. There must be something in the water these days. Perhaps I'll make a vacation from my trip to San Diego and enjoy the beautiful Fossil Fuel Lantern District.

San Diego would require at least two and a half hours drive from me in good traffic, so hungry for something other than fast food, I detoured to Julian, California, for a nice Turkey dinner and apple pie with ice cream on top. The town was among the first to be acknowledged when California became a part of the United States during the Gold Rush. Naturally, it stayed true to its roots aesthetically and remained unchanged, although there may have been an auto shop or two for your tractor. Once inside the restaurant serving the famous apple pie, I sat down to eat my pie when I overheard some local gossip.

"Hey, did you hear about the Aryan Cat Boy who went to see Mr. Harry Hatfield?"

"Yeah, he is a suspect, but if reports are accurate, where would a kid get ahold of something that could kill a man and not be caught in the act?

"Pretty sure the guy had state-of-the-art surveillance equipment with how rich he was."

"Maybe he did, still just when you think you know a guy.

"I remember when he was a baby and made catapults to fling food, he wouldn't eat at people."

"Never figured that would lead to an early life of crime."

"Hey, aren't we jumping the gun on this one?

"I mean, already a cat boy has made the news as a pariah for surviving a preschool collapse?

"How do we know this isn't some political media conspiracy to drive them to internment camps?"

I shuddered to hear "internment camps," as they were America's concentration camps to the extent we can believe those who came out of them. Even still, I shudder to think the United Planets wouldn't declare war on Earth if they did that. Speaking of which, I have a bad feeling about this. I stomached down the last of my food and went out to get some old-fashioned candies; while less uncommon back then, I can't find them in most candy shops in present-day for the road. The items consisted of a walking stick-sized bubble gum, those giant lollipops no kid can finish in one sitting, and licorice rope that one usually finds at Renaissance fairs, to name a few.

I headed back on the road for the rest of the trip, and when I got there, things seemed business as usual. I went to a fabulous mansion that most anyone would envy. I got there just as the police had finished questioning the cat boy who fit the profile the restaurant patrons slowly alluded to and wandered back to their vehicle.

"Boy, does news travel fast?

"I was just in Julian, and the locals already know Neko is a suspect."

The detective on the case was none other than Cat Sleuth.

"Ah, great to see you, Laila.

"I've heard much about you and your work back in Covina.

"For a new member, you sure are proving quite the investigator.

"Do not get cocky now.

"We have a pretty mixed bag with this one.

"Our primary suspect has just been questioned, but it does not add up."

"Well, Private Sleuth, can you give me the rundown of what has been found so far?"

"A bag of catnip classified as an illegal substance but is currently on the ballot to be legalized for medical use.

"What looks to be sniper rifle bullet wounds in vital organs, and nothing on the camera recordings shows who shot the gun but that it came in from his bedroom window."

"Any other complications?"

"Well, based on all the witness accounts, Mr. Aneko was coming for tea. "Billy Butler claims there was a fight over an arranged marriage of Mr. Aneko and Hillary Hatfield between Hillary Hatfield and the late Henry Hatfield. "Molly Morrison claims Hillary had the motive to kill her father to prevent the marriage and gain an inheritance.

"Ms. Hatfield claims that no one was in the room at the time of the shooting, which is consistent with the video feed."

"Wow, that is complicated.

"Did he perhaps fire anyone recently?"

"Our first suspect was recently terminated, Mr. Mc Coy.

"His entire IT team was outsourced to India, and he had a year left of term before he could collect a full retirement pension when he too was fired.

"Because they were fired and not laid off, they could not even collect a fraction of the retirement they had worked towards."

"Did you contact the company that set up the surveillance equipment?"

"Yes, because Mr. Mc Coy set it up for his boss, not to mention a lot of that around the city, we naturally suspected he might know something."

"And did you find anything?"

"Nothing that would link him to the crime, but we did find out it has blind spots in the bathrooms for obvious reasons."

"And about how far away can it see?"

"It can see anything on property and the sidewalk but nothing beyond the neighbor's fence."

"The attack most likely came from a sniper rifle or off the property."

"Yes, but the weapon was not registered when we traced the bullet back.

"So, assuming all local gun shops or means to acquire arms operated legitimately, it had to have been custom-made.

"Most likely by the perp themselves or a close friend.

"Besides Mr. Aneko showing up to visit the man for tea and appearing on the monitors outside the gates, why is he a suspect?

"Well, his family line is exceptionally gifted.

"They have the IQ to manufacture weapons out of common household parts.

"Mr. Mc Coy also has that capability, but there is no College University or Trade School record in the government database to suggest he had any experience making guns or other weapons to the level of a sniper rifle."

"If you know all this, why am I here?"

"Because according to the official records, you were an Agent of the UP long ago sent to Earth to help our kind to inhabit this world and live amongst us. "I was just one of the first generation to be born here and have no idea what lies beyond this planet.

"You, of all people, would know what is and is not possible given the level of technological know-how even the dumbest of the furry races possess.

"With that and, more importantly, your background studying forensic anthropology, you might find things we could overlook.

I skimmed through her computer database on the suspect's background.

"Public records show all suspects have no criminal background at all.

"No ties to any criminal families, just regular law-abiding citizens.

"I'd hesitate to consider this a case of a first time for everything, but it sure seems as much.

"Mr. Aneko does not appear to have much now, which is to be expected for one so young."

Cat Sleuth gave me the note that made the two individuals suspect in this case.

"Hmm, how careless of them.

"This note here is a threat from presumably the perp himself, but unless he was trying to be caught, which seems outright dumb, the letter is signed as if Mr. Aneko and Mr. Mc Coy, but the fingerprints on the document, no matter how many times I trace them do not match.

"They seem to come from an orphanage.

"Whoever was behind it must have hired someone to throw us off the path."

Suddenly I saw a strange-looking book written in Hebrew letters. I copied the title in my pocket notebook and entered it into my translator, "Book of the Loss did not open."

Stupid translator tools, I thought. I wonder what it could be. Suddenly a light flashed, and it was gone. I doubt my partner would believe me if I told him what I saw.

"Find out anything more, Laila?"

"Yeah, I traced the fingerprints, and according to our database, there are possible matches at an orphan home of 5 children who have recently been welcomed in.

"The DNA suggests it could be any of the five, and according to the public records I have accessed, each has a reason to want the man dead."

"One was an orphan whose parents could not afford them. A second was adopted because of insanity—the third by the death of all living relatives. Child protective services took away the fourth by intolerance of his sexuality and the fifth one.

"They all have one thing in common they did not get raised by parents who love them."

"So, you suggest that perhaps the intact and presumably loving family structure coupled with affluence may have driven someone to commit murder?"

"No, but I am saying that whoever is behind this could have paid them to throw us off their trail simply by being there and leaving their trace.

"With the circumstances surrounding them being put up for adoption, it seemed like the perfect cover-up."

"We'll send our forensic psychologist to get their statements and leads.

"Did you find anything else?"

"Nothing I could show, but I could use a day or two to relax after the cases I've worked on lately."

"Why is that?"

"Well, if you must know, I swore I saw something, but then it vanished as if it was never there.

"I figure the magnitude of the cases we've been working on lately has negative effects on the mind."

"Yeah, that is common for new workers. I also saw some pretty weird stuff on my first couple of cases."

"Like what?"

"Some kid with a scythe and book in his hand."

"When I rubbed my eyes, he was gone."

"Did you get a read on what the book said?"

"It was in broken Hebrew, and from best I could guess, it had something to do with death."

"I saw it too; I wonder what it could mean."

"I don't know, but there is nothing concrete to prove it wasn't a hallucination."

I scanned the bathroom. Indeed, the prints suggest Hillary Hatfield and the others were where they said they were. I began knocking on the wall to activate the hidden room button. Before I knew it, I was in another compartment of the Estate. Judging from all the dusty furniture, the owners had probably never used it. There were, however, some shoe prints leading into a Wardrobe. Cautiously I opened the wardrobe to find not someone waiting to kill me but what looked like some Ham Radio Device. I put gloves on, picked up the device, and knocked on the switch to exit the door.

"Find anything?"

"Yeah, I found an amateur radio device."

"Our suspect could have used this to keep in contact with someone without us tapping the lines."

"Yeah, but unless this plan was made months ago to happen on this exact day, it seems too dusty to have been used to communicate secrets recently.

"Still, the hidden room makes me wonder what kinds of skeletons the man had in his closet."

All jokes and pleasantries aside, it seemed odd that my partner and I saw the same thing best we could describe, yet neither of us could prove nor disprove its existence. Something unusual is a paw, but unless something concrete can link its relevance to this case, I should find it perfectly ethical to dismiss it as a hoax. We found evidence that could point to anything and analyzed it accordingly.

However, as we could find nothing conclusive to link anyone to the crime, we had to dig deeper. Our team had to take another approach, so we sent a man on our team for such an occasion—a land otter named Leonard Rudder-Butt. Don't laugh; that's his name. He's from

San Francisco, so it is not unusual to hyphenate a first or last name to include a second one. However, I wonder whose idea it was to have the family name Butt. Oh, wait, it is Rudder-Beaut sorry, my French is not that good. That's not important, though.

The following is information I received secondhand from him and compiled into a report for the courts. Bear in mind since these were minors, I am not allowed to give their real names were changed both in the record and this novel, as neither they nor their parents or guardians have permitted me even though they could be found in the glossary of the document I received. Not even their first names are real.

Location: Unwanted Bastards Orphan Home

Rudder-Beaut's Log code UBOH1 for log 1 of Unwanted Bastards Orphan Home. Today I interviewed five orphans sent there for different reasons, the first of which the parents couldn't afford. For their anonymity, we'll refer to the subject as Sheldon Shoeshine. The actual name has been kept secret for witness protection and can be found in the glossary in the back.

"Hello, Sheldon.

"How are you today?"

He didn't respond and was shivering, knowing I was a stranger and a person with a badge.

"I know this is hard, but I assure you this is nothing to worry about. I have some questions I want to ask."

"I-I didn't do it.

"I swear I don't even know why an agent of the police is questioning me!"

"We just want to find the truth to a critical case, and when we do, I'll be sure to give you a special gift for your cooperation."

"O-Okay... what do you want to know?"

"Are you familiar with anyone named Hatfield?"

"Y-yes... Mr. Hatfield used to come by here to bring us toys around the holidays and has given us a lot of money."

"And what about a Mr. Mc Coy?"

"Yes."

"What is he like?"

"He used to come alongside Mr. Hatfield, and the two were close even outside work."

"Did either act unusual the last time you saw them?"

Suddenly Sheldon shivered, looking more nervous.

"Stay with me, son.

"I need to know."

"If I tell you, I will die."

"Who said that?"

"Leeroy."

"Who is Leeroy?"

"Leeroy is an orphan like me, but he was sent here because all his family members died."

Remembering the name sounded familiar, and I asked him if he was what I'd refer to here as Leeroy London. He nodded, confirming my suspicions. We had a hell of a time trying to find their killer but ultimately determined the cause of death to be carbon monoxide poisoning. He was the sole survivor. He was punished and sent to the backyard tent for misbehaving. Inspection of the house suggested the dad tried to fix the heating system and did it incorrectly, having it blow an invisible gas as it warmed the home. Let that be a lesson hire a proper mechanic to work on your stuff, even if it looks like an easy fix.

"Well, he has been taken to the opposite end of the home so that he won't hear us here."

"Okay, the last we saw of Mr. Mc Coy, he seemed angry that his business partner had outsourced his company to India.

"He was holding some paperwork and spoke to Leeroy."

"And then what happened?"

"I couldn't get close enough to hear exactly what they were saying without being detected.

"I saw Mr. Mc Coy open a suitcase full of more money than we ever saw when talking to him."

"Hmm... That sounds very suspicious, indeed. I appreciate your cooperation. I think that will do."

I reached into my pocket and gave him a snow globe with cute kittens. His eyes lit up as he shook it and admired it. Next up was Leeroy. I wish my interview with him were as sweet as Sheldon, but I should have expected no less, as learning your parents died isn't easy, much less any siblings and relatives too.

"What do you want?"

"I want to know if you know a Mr. Hatfield or Mr. Mc Coy."

"What is it to you?"

"Mr. Hatfield is dead."

"Why should I care?"

"Because you could be a critical link to help us solve this case."

"I don't know nothing!"

"I think you do.

"You got a suitcase on you, don't you?"

"So does every orphan.

"If one doesn't keep an eye on their stuff, it'll get jacked."

"Especially if it has a boatload of money?"

He gulped a bit but then returned to a confident smugness.

"Inheritance."

"I don't buy it."

"You can't afford it."

"Listen here, you little punk.

"You could go to juvenile hall for a long time for obstructing the law, you know?

"Last I checked, they beat you little punks into a bloody pulp on day 1."

"A hell of a lot better than dying under mysterious circumstances..."

He covered his mouth and looked panicked.

"Aha!"

"Spill it!

"What do you know?"

He took a deep breath. His once cocky expression changed to one of resignation.

"Alright, Mr. Mc Coy offers me money if I convince the others here to touch many objects.

"Sounded like easy money, so, of course, we were in.

"None of us knew about the reason for touching them."

"And then what happened?"

"We heard a scream inside the nearby house, so we ran, not wanting to find out what it was about."

"Why didn't you just come out and say it then?"

"He vowed we'd never see it coming if we spoke any of this."

"Never see it coming?"

"Yeah, while talking with me, he told me what happened to my parents: it was carbon monoxide, an invisible gas that kills you in your sleep."

"We'll have police keeping watch of the area so you can sleep soundly tonight."

"That's a relief."

"There's just one other thing."

"Yeah?"

"Was anyone here given any pipe-shaped objects or other things he warned you not to point at each other?"

"Yeah, there was this gun, and it had some sort of binocular device on it."

I thought for a moment.

The unregistered weapon Lailah found at the scene of the crime.

Two possibilities, the gun they had was a decoy for the actual shooter, or two, one accidentally or intentionally shot him.

Never saw it coming.

Could this man have rigged the carbon monoxide alarms in this person's home and then made a deal with him?

We'd have found concrete evidence linking him to the crime if it was that open and shut.

None of this makes any sense.

"Just one last question, and we're done.

"Was anyone playing with the gun at any point when you all left your DNA on it?"

"Well... we were fighting over who would get to see through the scope."

"Who are we?"

"All five of us, Sheldon, Me, Peter, Sylvia, and Noe."

"So, you don't know which of you fired the round?"

"Yeah, we wrestled for it as kids do, not knowing it was loaded until boom!"

"Hmm... I think that will do.

"Can you tell Peter to come in?

"You're dismissed for now."

By this point in the interrogation, I'd understood if there was a shooting, it may have been accidental, but one also must question the chances one could hit someone by accident on the second floor of their home in their bathroom. I don't believe the guy was being entirely honest. They may have been playing with weapons they shouldn't, but whoever did this had to have been aiming somehow. But who... and why were they fighting over the gun? Was one of them trying to kill someone? I just had to know, but I needed to talk to someone sane first, so next was the one called Peter Power-Bottom. Yeah, he was gay, but that's his only reason for being put up for adoption. His parents were deeply religious, so you should know they'd not hold that as a dual last name combination.

A concerned but mostly likable demeanor orphan greeted me in the interrogation room.

"Hewwo, Sir."

"Hi, Peter, I take it?"

"That is correct."

"Okay, I heard from a couple of others that you all were involved in an issue involving a gun?"

"Oh yes, it was awful Silvia Syco and Leeroy London were fighting over who would hold the gun to watch the vantage point we were given.

"Sheldon and I were trying to break them up.

"Guns are not toys loaded or not."

"Indeed, they aren't.

"Good lad to understand that."

"Yes indeed... it's the one good value I got from my parents before they found out I was gay."

"Well, parents who are intolerant of other's true selves can eat a dick."

Naturally, this got a fit of laughter from the boy.

"Or take one.

"Oh, wait, they can't.

"It won't fit, hahaha."

"Right, well, I'm not at liberty to tell you how that works, but please tell me what the last thing was you saw before the big boom?"

"Well, Noe Hope had lept into the fray to get the gun away from Silvia Syco.

"A gun in the hands of someone with mental issues is always dangerous.

"The gun was pointing upward at about a 90-degree angle from best I could make of it.

"It was pointing diagonally upwards until it fired off its round.

"Then we heard the scream from afar that sounded like a man.

"We dropped the gun and ran for it."

"So, it sounds like either Noe or Silvia ultimately pulled the trigger."

"That's about the size of it."

"Very good I have what I need.

"Call Silvia in here, please."

With that, it was time to interview the last crazy one in this place if I wasn't after hearing their stories. A girl came in with the most psychotic expression you could imagine.

"You called for me?"

"Yes, I did, Silvia, I presume, so I understand you were involved in a gun accident?"

"You mean gun on purpose?"

"What?"

"Oh, don't be coy with me.

"I may be a girl, but I knew exactly what we were in for when we took this job."

"Go on..."

"We were to act as decoys while Mr. Mc Coy ended his former friend's life due to the loss of his job due to outsourcing."

"And how did that go?"

"Well, think about it.

"He'd been in enough times to see how we fight over toys at holiday times.

"Did he think we'd be any more responsible with guns?"

"So, you think the gun mishap was all part of his plan?"

"Get a bunch of pitiable orphans in just the right spot after monitoring your targets routines for days or weeks on end and let their nature take its course."

"As much as I hate to admit it, that sounds exactly like how it would have happened.

"With him knowing the security system's blind spots, it would have been easy to set such a thing up."

"Well, you're a lot smarter than I thought."

"I presume, coming from you, that's probably sarcasm."

"Any more questions?"

"No, that'll do.

"Please bring Noe in here."

If my dialogue wasn't apparent what I thought so far, I did not convey it very well. Nevertheless, exhausted as I was, I had but one more suspect to finish my report. A crying boy came in, looking way more scared than the others covering his head in fear.

"I'll tell you whatever you want, just don't hurt me!"

"Breath in and out, son, and tell me what happened the day of the big boom?"

He breathed meditatively after crying with my guidance and was finally ready to talk coherently.

"It was awful.

"Silvia attempted to shoot the gun in the distance without caring what she hit.

"I tried to stop her, but...

He sobbed in tears.

"I accidentally pulled the trigger, trying to wrestle it away from her."

"If it's any relief, you'll not be in adult jail for that.

"If what you say is true, the one who gave you the weapons is liable for accidents.

"As a minor as young as you are, you will probably be okay."

"I don't care about having to stay here knowing my parents hate me.

"Being taken away without a loving home is its prison.

"What upsets me is maybe if I had not tried to intervene, Mr. Hatfield would still be alive."

"That's a big maybe, kiddo.

"You could have saved many others in that house by intervening as you did.

"Either way, that's for the legal system to work out.

"I'm just a psychologist."

I didn't feel it right to interrogate this one further as I'd finally had enough data to piece together a likely scenario. So, I gave the poor kid a cookie and a juice box which he consumed with a tearful smile, but not the box itself. Then he told me something else. Something I was unsure how to ask without presuming guilt.

"I wonder what his plan would have been if he hadn't counted on us doing what we did.

"Could we have ended the man, or was it just a setup to distract from what happened?"

"I wonder the same thing, but absent any further clues, it seems accidental death is the conclusion we can draw.

"However, making unregistered weapons is legally contestable, and so is giving deadly weapons to minors, which they then accidentally use to harm another.

"Especially if it was part of the plan.

"That said, I thank you all for your time.

"You've all been helpful in our cause to solve this case."

After the interview, I took my notebook with me to Laila. She combined it with her forensic evidence to complete the case in San Diego Courthouse. Unfortunately, things had not gone as smoothly as we'd hoped. After being interviewed for the first time, it should come as no shock such a clever villain would have skipped town once the interrogations were completed. I'll let Lailah take it from here.

As suggested, Mr. Mc Coy was not around. We called every travel company he could have likely used to skip town and came up empty. Mr. Mc Coy possibly took off in a Yacht for another country and left the States. Still, he knew his sentence wouldn't be permanent, given the crimes we could pin on him so far. There must be more to this than we had imagined. Just what or who could be helping him stay a step ahead of us? Either way, I have a bad feeling about this. I got a text,

"Things are not as they seem.

"What you think is the villain may just be a patsy."

I didn't recognize the number but considered for a moment what evidence we had found to see if something was overlooked. The suspect seemed to have fled prosecution. So, the case went cold, at least for now.

CHAPTER 3

CHECK-IN CATASTROPHE

A Cat's Wrath Lasts Seven Generations

I could not have known this part of my story without talking to him, and I have opted to tell it from a third-person perspective based on some letters he sent me a couple of chapters from now and evidence found at the scene, and his age at the time.

Adam had, by this point, entered Elementary School. He didn't much care for the other kids, but as tumultuous as his home life could be, he at least had some nonhuman friends, and teachers were a mix of humans and furry species. Thankfully for us, all schools were quick to implement assistive technology. If our kind had not been accepted, humans would have lacked the technology for almost a decade or more. Therefore, Adam's difficulties with penmanship were not a problem. He could spell his words for tests in a source code generator as comments or plain text digital notepad without an autocorrect or spell-check instead of with pencil and paper. Access to the Internet would be turned off during these tests to prevent cheating. With these in place, Adam excelled where he would typically fail and gained new confidence in everything except Physical Education.

His Gym Teacher's name was Buzz Killington. He looked like a drill sergeant who had been discharged from the military with a mean streak that made one wonder how he got the job at an elementary school.

"Alright, maggots, to start the day, I want you all to drop down and give me ten push-ups."

Adam and the others did as commanded, but Adam couldn't get his upper and lower body in sync, so it looked like he was trying to mate with the ground, which elicited his peers' laughter.

"Damn it, Adam!

"This isn't a porn video, boy!

"Do them right!"

Adam stopped what he was doing, too embarrassed to do anything.

Adam was sent home looking depressed. Approaching the door to his home, he noticed it was open.

Adam thought to himself, *Odd, this door isn't usually open...*

He cautiously went inside the house. As he walked in, he felt something wet on his paws. He looked down to see it was a red substance. He shivered, remembering a dream about this a week ago.

No... it can't be...

Adam went upstairs, following the trail of blood. He turned right, opened his sister's room door, and shrieked. They hung back-to-back from each other on a noose. His teeth chattering and body quivering, he tearfully approached the door to his parent's room, where the blood trail lay. He saw the parents dead in bed with their throats slit. He screamed so loud anyone home at the time would have heard him. The weight of all he cared about was taken from him. The police showed up and escorted him away. Cat Sleuth began analyzing the evidence and sent it to our Forensics lab for analysis.

I, Lailah, had returned from my last case in San Diego. I looked at the remains and instantly knew who they were.

Adam... no... the poor boy suffered enough already being a scapegoat for murder once ...

I scrutinized the remains of the parents while Bill Benson came around,

"Everything okay in here?"

"Just business as usual, sir."

"I'm watching you, Laila.

"While your analytical skills are among the best in the business, I fear you still hold a lot of bias which could hurt upcoming cases.

"I should know.

"I was once in a similar position."

I acknowledged his point and returned to what I was doing.

Did I think to myself, *Why the sudden hostilities?*

Am I being sloppy, or is he afraid I will discover something I should not?

Bill Benson returned to his office, and I saw him from the corner of my eyes as he seemed to look at an image. I snooped in there a little later to discover it was a photograph of a happy family.

I heard him say, "If I were still in the military on the battleground, this would be the moment I would get shot dead."

After that minor distraction, I had an internal monologue.

The evidence on the bodies suggests the two sisters committed suicide, and the parents might have been asleep when it took place, but if that were true, Adam would have found them sooner.

What were they all doing before Adam got home?

I searched my pockets to see what I could find, which was the Hammer & Tail Construction Company card.

We arrested those criminals already, and their trial was open and shut.

Who all works for them?

Wait a minute..."

Images of past evidence rushed through my mind, the report about the hammer and tail construction company, the governor race before the incident, who funded the preschool, and the news account where Adam went on to talk of the hate Covina had for him, then what Bill Benson said about bias.

Could my boss have hinted that maybe the killer had some grudge or bias against Adam?

Then a list of specific people involved in the case flooded my mind, *Samantha Stockade, Lily Lockup, Judge Accurate.*

No, how ridiculous none of them could have orchestrated this so thoroughly and not left a trace.

Wait a minute...

I examined a murder weapon found in a parent's body. After running it in the system, I found it belonged to a Lily Lockup.

No way, she didn't!

I put the report through of what she had found. Before long, police were outside Lily Lockup's house and took her in for questioning as part of the investigation, but not before reading her Miranda rights. Inside the police station, Lily was wise and opted to have an attorney present for questioning. Silvester Shields was present for questioning on behalf of Lily Lockup.

This is how it went down:

Officer Stan Up began the conversation.

"Ms. Lockup, we brought you in today because we have reason to believe you may have been mixed in with a certain cat boy."

"Adam killed my family at a play a few years ago.

"What of it?"

"Not exactly.

"All evidence pointed to the negligence of those in charge of him and who had the place built."

"That is the biggest load of cow excrement I have ever heard."

"I would entreat you not to insult a sentient species within our department, as it is far from the point of why you are here."

Just then, an anthropomorphic cow came into the office outside the questioning room as if by comedic timing.

Silvester interjected, "Lily, as much as I know you hate the victim in this case, you will not be released from custody any sooner if you continue to act belligerent towards officers of the law, which as a lawyer, you are expected to respect."

"Fine, what do you want to know?"

Stan continued, "For starters, we found a specific item that belonged to you at the scene of the cat boy's home.

"It was covered with blood and led us to believe you may have had a hand in what went down.

"Care to explain?"

"What is the item?"

"It was a knife with your DNA and a special engraving."

Lily looked shocked, "I had lost that item while walking downtown to clear my head.

"It should come as no surprise that people like me need something to defend ourselves lest anyone we put away sick their friends on us."

"Go on."

"Well, I was walking down Grand Park in Downtown Los Angeles when a Lunar New Year parade occurred.

"Thinking it would be just the thing to clear my head, I stopped to watch it.

"As I did, someone rushed past me, collided with me, then kept running. "The person had a baby carrier on them, so I thought little of it.

"When I returned to my car, I reached for my keys in my pocket and touched my holster to ensure I had everything to find my knife was gone."

"Did you know what the person might have looked like, height, approximate weight, or any features that could be made out in a second?"

"I cannot remember. The one who ran into me looked like every other reveler in Little Tokyo."

"Then how was the only DNA on it yours?"

"People down there wear masks when sick and sometimes medical gloves.

"It is possible that with enough pairs of them, if not a single pair, no prints were left behind from them."

"I am not buying it, but there are no further questions."

"Can I go?"

"Unfortunately, in getting a warrant for your arrest, we expressed concern to the Judge you are too much of a flight risk, and you will have a hearing tomorrow.

"Despite this, the Judge has allowed a cash bail if you have the funds.

"I must warn you that bail for something like this costs millions.

"You would be as well to remain in your cell until we can have a fair trial for you if indeed you are innocent.

"Also, because you work with the Law, we will not place you with people you might have put away and will be treated like an officer who committed a crime."

In short, Lily reluctantly agreed that if she was innocent, bail would be a waste of money, especially since she had nowhere to go where she could get more work, so escape was not an option. At least, that was my sense of it, but I am not a Lawyer. How do I know this? Well, let's say I have friends in high places. You gain a certain level of trust when you are put on cases like these to try and find evidence so long as you will not be asked to testify, and neither are the ones who tell you it will not affect the outcome as long as you vow to secrecy.

This was the scene in the courtroom.

Judge Accurate took his seat, "Alright, we will now hear the case of Lily Lockup versus the U.S. Opening Statements, please."

Prosecutor Paul Padlock was the first to speak: "Your honor, what we have here is a case of revenge murder.

"Lily Lockup was furious about Adam going free due to insufficient evidence to link him to the crime."

Defense Attorney Silvester Shields spoke, "As much as I may have opposed my client in the past, I know for a fact she would not be so headstrong as actually to make good on such threats."

Judge Accurate nodded, "Alright, the evidence?"

Paul Padlock Presented it, "Exhibit A for Assault, the weapon the assailant used.

"Exhibit B for Battery and Biopsy, the findings from the victims' corpses.

"And Exhibit C the Report.

"According to the report, the parents were killed shortly after Adam got on the bus, the weapon is Lily Lockup's, and She recently adopted some children who we believe were involved in the killing of Mr. Hatfield.

"It would have been a perfect crime were it not for her weapon being used. "The Prosecution rests, your honor."

"And the defense?"

Silvester Shields responded, "Your honor, I am of the mind to say that if the weapon involved was Ms. Lockup's, the same evidence the prosecution brought forth will set my client free.

"We only need the witnesses to clear her name and the interview recording from the police station."

"An exciting claim indeed.

"Go on."

"I start by calling my first witness, Ms. Suki Yakimura, to the stand."

"Thank you for having me." She bowed respectfully.

"Ms. Yakimura, I understand you saw what happened on the day of the New Year Event?"

"Yes, I was attending my flower shop when out the window I saw the defendant seeming both troubled by something and trying to enjoy herself.

"I was about to offer her a complimentary cherry blossom sprout when a lady with a baby carriage bumped us both.

"I checked myself to find my wallet was still where it needed to be, so I thought nothing of the situation, and it seems Lily did too.

"I gave her the sprout as I intended, and she seemed happy.

"I did not see anything of interest after that."

Silvester Shields, "So you see, your honor, she can corroborate the story that Lily told the police in questioning."

Judge Accurate seemed intrigued, "I have listened to that tape in discovery, so from what I understand, Lily lost her knife that day.

"How does that relate to a killing that took place with it months later?"

Silvester Shields smirked, "Might I remind the court that her so-called begrudged one has more than just her as an enemy?

"Since Former Mayor Moneybags and his cronies were locked away, there has been an uptick in hate crimes on the furry kind.

"When we figure it takes more than racism alone to motivate one to act this way, it seems such powerful people could have indeed paid professionals to do the deed even behind bars."

Judge Accurate seemed outraged, "But that is impossible.

"We keep phone records on all prison calls in and out."

Silvester Shields did not seem phased, "Unless this was just one of many phases of a much bigger plan yet to be uncovered.

"But that is neither here nor there concerning my client's motives to do anything like that."

Judge Accurate seemed a little more confused than upset, "Then what is the point in such speculation?"

"That Lily Lockup was merely a victim of an unforeseen circumstance.

"While one might think she could have gone out and acquired yet another knife to do the deed, I happen to know the knife submitted into evidence is none other than a Hitler Youth Knife."

The entire courtroom was in shock and horror at that moment.

Lily Lockup looked defensive.

Paul Padlock shouted, "So she is a Nazi Sympathizer!

"She must have done it.

"Only Nazis wanted a pure Aryan race, and Adam threatened that!"

Judge, Accurate looking, ticked off again, "Order damn it all, I will have order!"

Silvester Shields, "No, her grandfather was a veteran and was gifted this knife by a grateful soldier.

"The item in question was recovered when liberating Jewish people and was discontinued in its current form for obvious political reasons.

"She could not have bought another one just like it and did the deed.
"Nor could whoever take it from her."

The Judge looked at it carefully to see that it had the Swastika and other features of a knife that had become standard.

"I hate to say it, but he is right.

"This weapon is too unique for her to have easily acquired another like it.

"Though of all the knives she could have carried, why this one?"

Paul Padlock narrowed his eyes, "But she still could have, and who else would hate him this much?

"How would a random stranger on the street know to take her knife and not anyone else's to do this?"

Silvester Shields nodded, "It does seem like the perfect crime, except we have reason to believe she had other enemies as well.

"Ones who might have had the motive to study her and be out for revenge.

"Does the name Thaddius ring a bell?"

Paul Padlock looked shocked, "Thaddius Yu?"

Silvester Shields nodded, "He was a top weaponsmith in World War II for the United States.

"He mainly made tanks and guns but also a paw full of Swords and knives.

"He disappeared one day, and few have seen him since.

"Her grandfather was his boss, and Thaddius could not make anything original.

"He resented him for being a cut above him in being able to make more unique things.

"With him already dead at the time it would have happened, murdering her husband would be the next best thing.

"I know this because Henry Skins babysat me and told me stories about the war from the departments he reported to throughout his career."

Judge Accurate groaned, "As much as I love stories, this is getting us nowhere.

"All physical evidence except the recordings and witness testimony points to her doing the deed.

"It is even her knife which even you do not deny.

"If nothing else is relevant here, I will turn to the jury for a verdict."

"I am sorry, your honor.

"I got nothing but theories on how it went down and no witness I could call upon… except one.

"I call Noe Lockup to the stand."

He was sworn in and nervous.

"Mr. Lockup, where was your adoptive mother on the day of the murder of Adam's parents?"

"She was home with all of us and left for nothing all day."

"You are sure about that?"

"She has been so busy being a mom to us and working on cases that she would have no time for much more than sleep."

"That will do."

"Anyone else to call to the witness stand?"

Both Attorneys shook their heads, indicating there was no one further.

"Alright, before the Jury Deliberates, let us hear closing arguments."

"As everyone can see, the defense has failed to produce physical evidence.

"Nothing beyond witnesses if that demonstrates Lily did not do what she is accused nor created reasonable doubt to suggest she could not have done it with outside help or on her own."

"And I say there is insufficient evidence that she, without a doubt, killed anyone.

"Further, the Prosecution failed to demonstrate she could not have lost a weapon unique to her or families of people who served."

"Has the jury reached a verdict?"

The Jury nodded and said, "Guilty as charged."

Judge Accurate nodded, "Then I sentence Lily Lockup to Life in Prison for four counts of first-degree murder."

He banged his gavel, and Lily was taken away screaming.

Silvester Shields looked defeated, "I tried so hard to prove she did not do it, but it convinced no one...

"What is worse is if I am right, the real killer is still at large, and who knows who they will target next."

After a decidedly long and tedious custody hearing, Adam lived with his grandparents on his father's side. While visiting the other parent's grandparents occasionally, he felt a little more at home with his father's side. He now lived in Michigan.

CHAPTER 4

VACATION DETESTATION

The Calm Before the Storm

While I cannot say I particularly mourned the imprisonment of Lily Lockup, I happen to know in times of hardship and grief; one can sometimes not be their best self. But there was a feeling I could not shake about all of this. Silvester Shields was onto something. Either that or the stress of our occupations meant we needed a vacation. And I am not alone. Even Cat Sleuth saw what should be impossible. Bones appeared where there were none at the former Covina Preschool. Even my boss is warning me I may be getting way out of my head. If I did not know any better, I would think he knew something he was not telling me. But I get paid vacation time, so maybe I should use it to unwind and maybe take training that could prepare me for what is to come. I went back to San Diego after the trial in Covina. I saw an unusual sight wandering the Fuel Lamp District of San Diego.

"Mr. Aneko?"

"You can call me Neko.

"Mr. Aneko was my father."

"Right, well, what brings you down here?"

"After being questioned in the case of Mr. Hatfield, I got a little inspired to create a sort of Mystery Game to help people sharpen their detective skills."

I raised a brow at this.

"A Mystery game, you say?"

"Yeah, I get a few people in a room, and they solve puzzles to unlock the final door and escape the place."

"Sounds like fun.

"Where might I find this Mystery Game?"

"Glad you asked.

"It is just off the 5 Freeway South of Carmel Valley, and cross streets are Pacific Mesa Blvd and Pacific Center Blvd.

"It is called 'Logic Brain Escape Room,' and I think you will like it."

Curious about this so-called "escape room," I called a few friends, including PI Patrick, Cat Sleuth, and Leonard Rudder-Butt, I mean Rudder-Beaut. When we got to the escape room, I saw a familiar face to the one I knew in Torrance.

"Welcome all to Logic Brain Escape Room.

"I am your host for the day, Sofer, which is Scribe in Hebrew."

"Odd question, but have I seen you somewhere before?"

"Maybe. I used to work at a drive-thru restaurant before I made my way down here.

"Anyways, for today's game, Neko has asked me to act as a character you can ask for hints at to help you escape.

"I will otherwise stand around looking pretty for the duration of your game as you activate the puzzle.

"Neko will communicate instructions through the intercom as you enter each room."

We signed our waivers and rule agreements to play this new game. For the theme, we chose what else but 'Logic Leap' themed around some of the most baffling but varied logic puzzles known to man.

"You all have entered this puzzle room.

You get precisely one hour to solve all of these puzzles and escape.

“There is an emergency exit button should someone have a medical emergency but using it will not be considered a win but a forfeit.

“The point of the game is to solve puzzles to exit the place.

“Good luck, and be sure to yell ‘The Pen is Mightier Than the Sword’ for a hint.”

Sofer waited for us nearby as Patrick, Leonard, and Cat looked around the first room and began picking up objects, hoping to find where they go and any hints. The room looked like a Number Puzzle, so I was already out of my element a bit. Luckily it seems Leonard took a psychological approach to decode the numbers.

“From best I can tell, the object of this number game is not to have any rows of numbers duplicate in columns or rows as you use numbers 1-9.

“We have 81 squares and some prefilled numbers in a 9x9 grid.”

In short, it took Leonard 15 minutes to solve the number puzzle. I surmised he does this often, as I could sit on one of these for hours and be stumped depending on difficulty. He found a key and unlocked the next door while Sofer followed us.

“In this room, you see two statues representing guardians guarding two doors.

“Hit the button and ask them but one question to find your solution.

“One guard always lies.

“The other always tells the truth.

“One door leads to the next room, the other to doom.

“To unlock the right door, you must ask the correct question.

“For legal reasons, we cannot hurt you for taking the wrong door. “You just end up back where you began.”

Luckily, word-based puzzles are my specialty, so I approached the console and pressed the button to ask my question. “If you were the other guy, what would you say is the correct door?” They both point to the left door and both the left and right doors open.

I led my team to the door on the right, and we were in the next room. We saw a game show stage and had forty minutes left on our clock. Cat Sleuth took on this next one.

"You are on a game show and are presented with three curtains.

"Two contain a goat, and one has a car.

"Assume you want the car and select a curtain.

"The game show host opens one curtain you did not pick to reveal a goat. "You are presented with two options: switch your curtain or stay with your choice.

"If you think you should switch, crank the lever on your left as you face the stage.

"If you think you should stay, use the lever on your right."

Cat Sleuth activated the lever on the left, and the next room opened. "That was easy.

"You see, most people think you have a fifty-fifty chance regardless of whether you switch, but actually, you increase your odds of getting the car if you switch."

We proceeded to the next room.

"For your final puzzle, you have three objects on the same side of a river one is a box of cabbage, another is a sheep, and the last is a wolf.

"You need to get all three across the river.

"You may only take one at a time in your boat without them eating each other before you get all three across."

PI Patrick looked at the objects on one side of the room and seemed stumped.

"The pen is mightier than the sword!"

Sofer bowed respectfully, "You may return objects from one side to the other as needed to account for predator and prey relationships."

Suddenly the PI figured it out. He first took the sheep across and then went back for the wolf. He then took the sheep back with him as he left the wolf on the other side. Then he grabbed the cabbage box and took it to the other side, then he grabbed the sheep back from the original side, and the key dropped in front of us. I picked it up and unlocked the door. We had just thirty minutes left when we stopped the clock and triggered a victory confetti effect followed by happy music. Out of custom, we picked up a bunch of signs with silly slogans for a group photo at the end.

Neko came out excitedly. "Congratulations, you all are responsible for solving this room the fastest."

Sofer also said, "Yeah, when we were testing the rooms, I could not develop the solution for the Sudoku.

"Most people fail there and are unable to proceed.

"The other puzzles are fairly easy by comparison."

I said, "Well, Neko, I think you should call this a hard-level room or make the sudoku so painfully easy that it can be solved by just entering one number in each nine-by-nine grid."

"Suggestion noted, these games are supposed to be more about teamwork and using each other's skills than necessarily being experts at anything.

"However, this specific room is meant to help a team hone logic skills needed by investigators, which is why I recommended it to you.

"Our other room, 'Scribes Sanctum,' is much easier and tests more your ability to spot subtle things that appear out of place, such as a Viking rune in the middle of a Hebrew Alphabet."

Sofer smiled, "I designed that one myself as I enjoyed visual and text-based puzzles as a kid."

I nod, "We will have to try that one sometime, but I think we need to rest our brains a bit after that last one."

"No problem, come back anytime."

We left the place and went back to our hotel room. As fun as that was, my sixth sense told me we might need these skills we honed sooner than we thought.

It was eerily quiet when I woke up next like you could hear a pin drop. Need I remind you, as a fox, I have an enhanced sense of sound beyond what a human could pick up? If there were something at or around the level of a dog whistle noise, I would hear it. I went down the stairs, and there was no person to be found in the entire hotel. Not a bellhop, front desk clerk, or even customer waiting to check in or out to be found.

How weird should they have some hotel staff down here, right?

"Hello?"

My voice echoes far and wide, but no response.

Unreal to think I could be in a now empty building.

Did I even check in last night?

Does this place even exist?

In hopes I might find anyone who could explain what was happening, I tried the front door, but it would not budge.

Well, now what am I supposed to do? I cannot leave unless I jump the building, assuming any doors beside my room work in this dump or the windows.

If I did not know any better, I would think I had entered some paranormal maze.

Nothing to do but see what opens, I guess.

I began knocking on doors and anything that might draw the attention of any living beings.

No answer.

This is impossible.

I cannot possibly be trapped here with no one to talk to, nothing to eat, and nowhere to go.

As if sensing my hopelessness, a black cat appeared seemingly out of nowhere.

How cute, but do I imagine it out of stress, or did I not see it this whole time?

The cat slowly trotted down a path I just went. With no other leads, I followed it. It opened a hidden door behind a bookcase, and to my relief, I found Leonard Rudder-Beaut there.

"Leonard!"

"Hey, Lailah, you wake up like this too?"

"Yeah, I began my daily routine to find no trace of life here."

"Quite peculiar indeed."

"Yeah, all doors except the one I have access to were locked.

"No other beings could hear me when I knocked, and suddenly this black cat came out of nowhere and led me here."

"I may not be much of a detective, but it sounds like none of us have had a psychological anomaly as much as a temporal one at best."

"Go on."

"Well, if this were all in our heads, it seems highly improbable we would be able to meet given the lack of others in the building.

"You have heard of the Bermuda Triangle, no?"

"Yes."

"Then you know things have disappeared historically, be it planes, people, and whatnot."

"Yeah, but what does that have to do with San Diego?"

"Well, if something like that can happen there, perhaps this building could have its hidden passages or places one can wind up if luck is with them."

"Seems a bit farfetched, but I cannot refute it absent any other evidence."

"Well, we won't get any closer to an exit if we do not consider the type of problem we have and how we can solve it.

"We were just in an escape room.

"Try and think like you designed one and ask yourself, 'where would I hide a key to get through?'

"And 'what clues might I leave behind either intentionally or not?'"

"Hmm, maybe in one of the books on a shelf?"

I pulled down a relatively thin book called "Into the Mind Out to Nature Musings of An Interesting Man."

"Hmm, weird, it looks like a book of poems."

"Ah, excellent there will surely be hints if you know how to interpret their meaning."

"Hmm 'he Lurks?' What sort of clue could I possibly divulge from that?"

"Maybe not that one; try digging deeper."

"Hmm, conformists get out?

"No.

"Oh! 'A grave situation' now we might have something."

"I knew you would see it too."

"The words suggest a child has died, but I know it cannot be that simple.

"Wait, when we become adults, the child in us dies.

"Could we be looking for a children's book or toy?"

Searching past the bookshelves, I found a child's twin bed. I investigated it to find nothing conclusive, but my sixth sense remembered the poem and thought I should lie in it. I lay in it, and another door opened, and I found PI Patrick in what else but a cardboard box. In case you forgot, I implied he had difficulty finding his way out of a cardboard box in chapter 1.

"Hey Lailah, funny you should find me here in this box.

"I do not know why, but I feel a sense of inner peace while in it."

"That is all well and good, but I think I speak for Mr. Rudder-Beaut and me when I say that we should work together to get out of here."

Leonard nodded affirmatively as PI Patrick got out of his box.

This room seemed pretty dim in the lighting department, but being animals, we could all see well enough without flashlights.

On the wall were some words that could be made out.

On the darkest day, in the dimmest light, find the item which gives comfort tonight.

We put our heads together, and the PI had a good idea for once.

"I am not a child psychologist, but perhaps a teddy bear or night light is what we should find."

Leonard nodded approvingly. We found a glow-in-the-dark teddy bear as we scoured the many plush dolls and stuffed animals. We held its glowing form up to the hint, and it revealed an invisible ink message.

You figured it out with mental might, and now you see the door is to your right.

We look right to see a door that looks like a toy block set. Without hesitation, I open the door to the next room and find Cat Sleuth in what appears to be a number and alphabet room. It had what appeared to be Nordic Runes, Hebrew Alef Bet symbols, and English crossword puzzles in addition to Sudoku.

"Lailah, there you are! Leonard! Patrick too!"

"Cat! Great to see you."

After a brief reunion, we agreed that this room would be the hardest because it seemed to rely on our unique skills.

Cat Sleuth pulled out his trusty notepad, "I will write down any clues you find for this, as it seems the best use of my skills.

"If I had to guess, you should look for things that fall out of the pattern in these puzzles."

We nod and take our positions. PI Patrick began examining for random objects that might help us decipher things while Leonard took on the Sudoku, and I tackled the Different Alphabets and word scrambles.

"Cat, this Sudoku has already been solved but incorrectly."

"Tell me the incorrect numbers."

"20, 15, 19, 15 again, 12, 22, 5, 20 again, and 8."

"Hmm, since Sudoku does not use numbers higher than 9, perhaps we should match them to letters of the English Alphabet.

"Wait, 5 and 8 are wrong?"

"They intersect with other numbers invalidly according to the rules. "Specifically, you cannot have repeat values in the same row, and the font on they were penned in there and not part of the ones the puzzle gives you.

"So far, if we convert them to the letter of the English alphabet based on the order of letter appearance, we get, 'To solve t-h.'

"Perhaps the other puzzles will help us finish the sentence."

I examined the crossword puzzle circled all valid words, and yelled out my findings of unused letters, "e, r, o, another o, m."

Cat nodded, "To Solve the room."

I then looked at the Nordic runes and found some Hebrew ones mixed into them. Applying the same logic as the Sudoku, I matched them by the number on the Aleph Bet chart.

"13, 14, 22, 1."

"Any special markings on the vowel?"

"Yeah, a dot over the aleph."

"That word is Hebrew for Find.

"We have 'To solve the room find.'"

The last part was much harder to find, but, using my trusty translator from Viking Runes to English, off of the words that did not have a Hebrew letter intersect them, the last words converted from Elder Futhark to English, I yelled, "The sin."

Cat wrote it and read aloud, "To solve the room, find the sin."

I looked all over the walls to see if the Hebrew letter "Sin" was anywhere, it should not be, and as if by G-d itself, I found a paper that listed the sins Jewish people repent for on Yom Kippur via the Viddui with the letter "sin" on the top of it.

On the back, it read, *Excellent work solving these puzzles.*

To open the next door, place the blocks that have now become visible into the indents of each wall. You have a visual of the sin they represent as per the Ashamnu to help you.

"Well, PI, want to do the honors of finishing this puzzle?

"You need not be literate in any language for this one."

I broke the fourth wall and turned to the reader as if to tell them a secret, "If you do not want to read all the sins, you may skip it for the outcome by turning to the page until you no longer see Hebrew.

"Due to varying e-reader screen sizes, I cannot predict the page across all devices, but print editions should see the outcome on the bottom of Page 57, according to the digital proofreader.

"Otherwise, prepare yourself for a list of sins Jews repent for every Yom Kippur."

My teammates looked at me funny as if thinking I had gone off the deep end, but then shrugged, not wanting to press the question.

Patrick began by lining up the blocks and pictures corresponding to the sins as follows:

אָשַׁמְנוּ Ah-sham-noo (We have trespassed [against God and man, and we are devastated by our guilt]) a picture of someone walking past a no trespassing sign looking remorseful.

בָּגַדְנוּ Bah-gahd-noo (We Betray) with the picture of a rogue stabbing a man in the back wearing the same symbol.

גָּזַלְנוּ Gah-zahl-noo (We have stolen, we have slandered) with a picture of someone stealing from another person. Yet another image was of someone smirking while facing another person as if to speak lies to them

דִּבַּרְנוּ דֹּפִי Di-bar-nu do-fi (We have used our mouths for speaking truth and evil) A person whispering a secret with a picture of another person in a talking bubble. Both are smirking.

הֶעֱוִינוּ Heh-eh-vee-noo (We have caused others to sin) matched to an image of someone being whipped into misleading another.

וְהִרְשַׁעְנוּ Vih-heer-shah-noo (We have caused others to commit sins for which they are called wicked) with a depiction of someone being armed for war in armor, one might expect of a black knight in medieval times.

זַדְנוּ Zahd-noo (We have sinned with malicious intent) was placed with an image of a villain of a mustache-twirling cartoon villain.

חָמַסְנוּ Chah-Mahss-noo (We have forcibly taken others' possessions even though we paid for them) is next to a picture of a person clinging to a plush bear with a person offering a vast sum of gold for it.

טָפַלְנוּ שֶׁקֶר Tah-fahl-noo sheh-kehr (We have added falsehood upon falsehood; We have joined with evil individuals or groups) matched to an image of a group of people in black concealing cloaks.

יָעַצְנוּ רָע Ya'atznoo rah (We have given harmful advice) near a picture of a mafia loan shark.

כִּזַּבְנוּ. לַצְנוּ Kee-zahv-noo lahtz-noo (We have deceived; We have mocked) placed near a picture of a child pointing and laughing at another.

מָרַדְנוּ Mah-rahd-noo (We have rebelled against God and His Torah) is a picture of an x mark on an open scroll that resembles one of the dead sea scrolls.

נִאַצְנוּ Nee-ahtz-noo (We have caused God to be angry with us) is an angry face image.

סָרַרְנוּ Sah-rahr-noo (We have turned away from God's Torah) A man facing his back to an open Ark holding scrolls for worship.

עָוִינוּ Ah-vee-noo (We have sinned deliberately) a man eating a boar's head.

פָּשַׁעְנוּ Pah-shah-noo (We have been negligent in our performance of commandments) A man working with a clock behind him that said 'Friday 9 pm.'

צָרַרְנוּ Tzah-rahr-noo (We have caused our friend's grief) An angry drunk wearing a matching t-shirt to him who seems saddened by his friend's state.

קִשִּׁינוּ עֹרֶף Kee-shee-noo-oh-rehff (We have been stiff-necked, refusing to admit that our sins cause our suffering) A scene of intervention of loved ones near an annoyed-looking man.

רָשַׁעְנוּ Rah-shah-noo (We have committed sins for which we are called [raising a hand to hit someone]) is a picture of someone about to be punched in the face.

שִׁחַתְנוּ Shee-chaht-noo (We have committed sins resulting from moral corruption) A person wearing orthodox attire willingly gives money to a criminal as if a bribe.

תִּעַבְנוּ Tee-ahv-noo (We have committed sins which the Torah refers to as abominations) A picture of someone committing self-harm.

תָּעִינוּ Tah-ee-noo (We have gone astray) A picture of someone driving a car in the opposite direction of a one-way street sign.

תִּעְתָּעְנוּ Teeht-ah-noo (We have led others astray) A picture of a person conducting a group away from a view of a city behind them into a desert towards them.

The final key dropped, and I noticed it had an Alef Symbol on it in a way that made it read as Aish or a meditative breath in Kabbalah. I inserted it into a door with a painting of a relaxed-looking Rabbi above it that opened due to Patrick's careful placement of the sins. When we went outside to the front lobby, a crowd cheered, and a person dressed as a game show host happily emerged from hiding.

"Congratulations, you have completed our international hotel game show challenge, 'Empty Inn.'"

"Because of it, each of you has won a completely comped hotel stay for as long as you are here and one million united states dollars to be split equally among the four of you."

I was in disbelief.

"What? But we did not sign up for this."

"Do not worry.

"It was no purchase necessary as you could have entered by signing up at our table near the convention area while paying nothing to attend.

"You just got lucky and were entered by a lot drawing of people staying here, which was mixed into the free entries to give an equal chance of selection.

"All you have to do is sign the consent to be on TV and not hold us liable for this surprise, and the money is yours."

Not one to be a fool, I carefully analyzed all print on the contract brought before us to see that they could be sued for falsifying this contract in any way as well as the prize offered. However, they reserved the right to make us look silly on TV for ratings. We huddled together to decide if we were all okay with this. To make a long chapter short, we did not particularly care what others thought of us as our jobs were neither top secret nor exposed in any way by what we did or said.

CHAPTER 5

CARRY ON MY WAYWARD SON!

He Doesn't Cry Anymore

After an albeit twisted vacation where my team found ourselves in an escape room and an escape game show prank, we were unprepared to be on something that lingered on my mind.

Why is all the weird stuff happening to me and those I associate with?

Why can't I take a vacation without something weird happening?

Moreover, I hope the people I handled the cases with are in a better place now.

Just then, I saw Silvester Shields.

"Hey, Silvester, how are you doing?"

"Not so good after that stunt back in the courtroom. I am under investigation and may be disbarred for my court conduct."

"I feel it. I may not like Lily Lockup, but something tells me you were onto something."

"Oh?"

"Yeah, that oddly specific weapon used in the murder, the fact that someone would have had to have served or knew someone who did to acquire it without stealing it.

"Problem is it can be a real kangaroo court scenario when controversial evidence comes up, even if it should get someone off the hook."

Just then, a Kangaroo wearing a judge wig, Gavel, and other apparel a judge would wear in movies hopped by us.

"No offense Kang Roo."

"None taken."

Seriously the politically incorrect happenstances are becoming ridiculous at this point.

"Tell me about this, Thaddius Yu. What do you know?"

"Well, besides his name meaning 'heart,' seems like an oxymoron if you saw his devices on the battlefield.

"He was an absolute machine in making them.

"Any model you could think of, he would work tirelessly to make it.

"It is like all he could do was copy what exists."

"Hmm, that is very interesting. So why do you think Thaddius might be behind this?"

"Besides jealousy as a motive brought up in court, he lacked empathy or compassion for anyone.

"It did not matter if they were higher or lower in rank.

"To him, the ends justified the means, no matter who died or got dismembered.

"What is unclear is why he would do this.

"Who could pay him to make these seemingly disconnected cases go off without a hitch and always stay above us all?

"If I could have made a fleshed-out theory, maybe Lily would be doing no time."

"It is not your fault.

"Some cases are impossible to create sufficient doubt to get people off the hook.

"I hope one day we get to the bottom of this and find the truth."

"Without a search warrant, any hope of finding concrete evidence that cannot be thrown out in court is lost.

"Unlawful search and seizure is the law, and I shudder to think we would break the law as old as this country."

"So, we have one suspect.

"I am a little wary of Bill Benson.

"Lately, the more crimes and binds I get myself out of, the more hostile he becomes to my supposed carelessness.

"I do not know much about him other than he used to be a detective too, so if anyone knew how to cover their tracks, it would be someone who worked with him.

"That still leaves the question if he or someone close to him did this... why?

"Surely someone like those two would be the first anyone would suspect in unsolved case files if they read their share of mystery fiction.

"And what about Sofer?

"Seems weird he would suddenly jump ship from fast food and go down to San Diego to work an escape room.

"Don't get me wrong, loads more fun, but how would they make rent off that alone with it being a new industry?

"Then again, how would they have in fast food as a cashier?

"Then there is Neko and that Prank Game Show Host.

"Yeah, the money is legit in the latter case, but the prank's odds and difficulty seem too well thought out to be a coincidence.

"But nothing in those rooms could have killed us.

"Were they testing us?

"Neko is a cat boy passionate about puzzles and whatnot, but why would he?

"And then Adam?

"None of this makes any sense."

"Don't overthink it.

"Sometimes, the simplest explanation is the best one.

"And hey, maybe Lily, in a fit of insanity, really did kill this guy's parents.

"It would not be the first time someone melted down and did the unthinkable in distress."

"Bill is right.

"My biases and theories are driving me up a wall.

"I need to take these cases as they come without regard to the bigger picture.

"Then my answer will come when it was meant to come."

"It happens to all of us at some point."

I went home to find a curious letter from a familiar suspect. How weird I do not remember giving them my address, and they must have got it from the phone book. It was from Adam, and it read as follows.

Dear Lailah,

I hope this letter finds you well. You may be wondering how I got your address when last you saw me; it was a hotel. Well, it was on the white pages of a phone book. Perhaps it slipped your mind to remove yourself from it, but that is unimportant.

I now live in Michigan with my dad's parents, and I am mostly picking up life as usual. None of the kids know what happened in Covina, and I have opted to pretend my grandparents are my parents, as those my age likely won't question it until they are much older.

It is no business of theirs anyway. It would be nice to keep in touch since you seem rather amusing, and I find it helpful to deal with issues if I have someone to write letters to.

Letters, while slow, make for an exciting break from routine. If you prefer not to write to me, I understand, and if you do, I will try and slip fun stickers I pick up into the envelope each time.

Sincerely,

Adam

P.S. Let me pull the lever on the chair when you find out who killed my parents.

I shivered at that last statement, like somehow this was just too in character for him despite the fact he had never hurt a soul. I suppose everyone grieves differently. Still, he may be right. Now that I do forensic work, I am a sitting duck as long as my name and address are on the white pages. I took a step without looking below me to hear a pained quack. Yes, a duck was sitting before me, and I stepped on it. Seriously I have to wonder if any of this is real when it seems like every time I use a colloquialism for an animal, it happens. That is another thing, though. Not even Adam thinks Lily did it, even though she hates him. Adam may be a child, but children do not usually have that level of critical thinking. What could he know about the situation? Did Adam make any enemies in school? Also, he seems to have adapted too well to the change. Adam did mention premonitions of what would happen to his school. Could he have seen this too? I better write back and see what I can learn, but I must be subtle if I want honest answers.

Dear Adam,

Hearing you adapt well to your new home and life is a pleasant surprise. Write to me if it is ever complicated or if you need someone to vent to. I may not be able to respond instantly, but I can send you encouragement when you need it.

Have you had any interesting dreams or thoughts you would like to share? I may not look it, but it has been years since I was a kid, so I am curious about what thoughts one might have. I still remember when we met. Sad it had to be under such unfortunate circumstances. Then again, the enemy of my enemy is my friend, I guess.

Moreover, in the last letter, you said that when we find who killed your parents, let you pull the lever. What did you mean?

Sincerely,

Lailah

A couple of weeks passed without much happening beyond lab work, and relatively easy to solve cases that hardly needed me. Then I got a letter back.

Dear Lailah,

Thank you for writing back. I will happily vent if anything comes to mind. It seems my cover of not having birth parents is working quite well. I made a few friends, and we have visitations periodically. They will know the truth when the time is right, but I would not think it a good idea, given how judgmental kids can be at my age.

To address what I said before, I do not think Lily Lockup killed my parents. She may be angry at me and possibly insane, but she is not stupid. If she were to try something like this, she would have used a weapon anyone could have had to create reasonable doubt. She was set up, but I do not know by who.

Though I suspected what happened to the preschool and that my parents would be found dead like they were, those visions never produced a culprit or any features of who did it. It is always some figure whose form is distorted by darkness.

Perhaps this is how I steeled myself for what was to come. I knew no authorities would believe me if I told them a vision told me my parents were going to die, and I did not even have a time frame of when. So, realizing it was inevitable, I prepared my wishes of whose side I would stay on, and with my mom's side being a bit of a mixed bag from what I knew of them, it was a no-brainer.

I still write to Great Grandma, though. She seems to understand what it is to have the gift of words and seek answers.

That said, I realize a standard mode of death for murderers is the electric chair, so I would happily avenge my family once they catch the one who has done it. Though, I won't act illegally to do it, and it is not how I want the departed to remember me, nor am I in a hurry to join them.

Still, I leave the light on for them. It makes no logical sense, but if there is an afterlife, maybe my light will help them find their way.

Sincerely,

Adam

That was the end of the relevant exchange here. The rest of the letters were primarily regular topics of school or travel and entertainment topics. Still, I just about cried hearing Adam would leave the light on for his parents. Not for any hope they would be back, but to help them navigate forward. It would appear the most rational do not believe Lily Lockup did the deed, not even Adam, so maybe I am not crazy to think this is all a conspiracy. I do not know what to do against the chaos brewing across the board, and there is no shortage of cases. I have had at least five of them each year since I began, and only one is worth writing about here.

Eventually, the letters slowed to a halt, but I thought little of it since he was probably getting more and more homework, and thus free time was more limited.

Besides working on cases, I occasionally get out with the team, but our enjoyment is usually short-lived. One particular outing of note was when we all went to the Clops Deli, Bakery, Restaurant, and Bar in the North Fairfax area of Los Angeles. We were all seated around a table, exchanging stories of how we came to work for FI 310, as we abbreviated it. I kicked it off.

"I used to be a nurse and contemplated getting into hospice care, but I also considered forensic nursing.

"It always seemed so cool based on the TV shows of it, but I never quite knew how I would go about being one or if it was worth pursuing.

"But we live in a country where a person working as a research scientist could become a nurse, or a Businessman become a Lawyer.

"Little could I have figured I had the kind of background for this type of work.

"Kids loved me, though, as I always kept toys of courage to help them get through their surgeries.

"That is where I first met Adam before the preschool burned down. He was a good kid, but none of that matters in a world that hates as much as ours.

"Ultimately, I went the Forensic Anthropology route and got my fast-track certifications instead of degrees."

PI Patrick Nodded, "Not to suggest any lack of qualifications on your part, but I think necessity played a role in the process seeing as how agencies like ours are in high demand and few have the stomach for it, much less the index.

"Were it not for that, you would probably never get to leave the forensics lab except to testify or as an expert witness."

"So, how did you become one of us, Patrick?"

"Well, I am sure you are familiar with the Vietnam War?"

"Yes."

"I had no choice in the matter.

"All male humans were subject to the draft.

"I was one of the few who knew you were a furry before your lot could freely roam without human disguises, as you may recall."

"Yes, and I know you had difficulty escaping things that seemed trivial to me."

"Anyways, I survived the war, but part of me wishes I did not.

"When I returned, people treated me no better than Adam when they thought he killed many kids.

"Only it was worse.

"We killed people in that war.

"Our enemies were not all trained adults either.

"Child soldiers were forced by their government to serve.

"My fellow soldiers and I were seen as savages and murderers rather than proper veterans who were forced to fight a war few of us gave a rat's ass about.

"My wife and kids all left me, and if not for this job here, I would have nothing.

"Some souls were even less lucky than me.

"Before then, I was studying cybersecurity, but I was not the best at test taking, so I did not make the military's cut, and no big tech firms felt all that compelled to try me out due to my war history well as lacking skillset.

"I was always more hands-on when proving what I knew.

"Sometimes I think Bill keeps me here more out of pity than qualifications."

I gave him a sympathetic look, "I am so sorry. I could never know what it is to go through all that."

Bill Benson chimed in next, "That is not true.

"You have a broad mix of skills that could make you an asset to the team.

"Sometimes a case calls not for a specialist but a generalist who can assemble the pieces and see how it all relates.

"As for my experience, I may not look it, but I served in World War II.

"There, I made some connections that I keep to this day, and I came to learn about some potentially problematic people.

"I could have retired by now, but in light of the Civil Rights Movement, I saw a higher calling.

"I was once a Forensic Investigator for the police force, and as case volumes became more than any in-house investigative team had the workforce to handle, I split off and formed my own Private investigation company.

"Some I knew had a good head on their shoulders and were hired onto some of the other units.

"Other companies soon followed suit, and it was not long before the UP sent help to us, knowing that the nature of our work was in their interests since it involved the safety of the furry races that have made Earth home."

"So how is it you remain so youthful despite the fact you should be well into your 70s, if not 80s?"

"I made a deal with the UP that if they supplied me resources to investigate cases, I would do everything in my power to protect all furry personnel of interest to them.

"I, however, was not immortal, so I could only keep that promise as long as I was alive.

"The representatives of the UP seemed to have read between the lines and took me to a fountain of youth where I was to submerge until I could pass for someone in their early 20s.

"Besides pulling off the look, I feel just as spry as I did back then.

"So, Lailah, I suppose I could ask you the same since I know you had to have been around well before the 1960s to have known PI Patrick as a kid."

"Well, that is a good question, I am not sure if it was ever disclosed to you, but those who were born of those who used the fountain of youth have the side effect of looking a specific age for quite a while.

"For example, if Adam was born of people who used it, even if not direct descendants, he could pass for someone in middle school or younger, well into his early 20s.

"Likewise, I look maybe 25 because my family had used it before I was born.

"Because of this, furry races can live hundreds or perhaps thousands of years, provided forces do not slaughter us outside of aging."

"Interesting indeed.

"So, what will that mean for me?"

"No idea.

"We had never had a human use the fountain of youth before, so you could wind up being immortal as far as aging, or you could just end up extending your life to about 200 years.

"Consider yourself our test case."

"That is calming."

"What about you, Leonard Rudderbeaut?

"You have been waiting patiently to tell your backstory."

"Well, you both seemed to have interesting stories.

"While mine is not as exciting, maybe as yours, I took a keen interest in criminal psychology from a young age.

"I could never quite grasp what drives a person to take another's life, and I found myself interviewing death row inmates while studying it.

"I quickly realized from my curious case studies that many start young, and only a fraction of them is driven to it by events in adulthood.

"As a result, I dual majored in Criminal Psychology and Child Psychology in college well into Graduate School.

"Because of the criminal nature of Criminal Psychology, it should go without saying I had a few more criminal law courses than most Psychology majors.

"I also try to lend insight into the process when I suspect a child is innocent or undeserving of some of the harsher sentences that would be handed to an adult.

"The sad trend I see is a lot of the children I work with are very intelligent but were not given a fair chance in life.

"Bill had seen my work with children as a Mental Health Advocate and hired me to work with this unit."

I mused, "So two of us have experience with children and two with war.

"What an interesting pattern."

Cat Sleuth said, "I was an avid reader of Mystery Novels and always wanted to be a detective.

"I majored in criminal justice and minored in English, where I chose to take novel writing and Communications.

"For as much as Bill scoffs at mystery fiction, I get the sense he has a few guilty pleasure reads or perhaps prefers the existing visual mediums.

"Why do I think this?

"Well, after writing a few crime thrillers that were perhaps a little too real for some, he came to one of my book signings and offered me a job doing actual detective work.

"I was a Paralegal at the time as the book writing was only modestly successful.

"I made pretty good money as a Paralegal and could have become a judge or politician, but it left a bad taste in my mouth to be expected to lie, so Bill Benson offered me a competitive salary to work for him instead as a Detective."

Bill Benson said, "Finding entertainment in Mystery Fiction and insight into criminal minds is one thing, but presuming that criminals will realistically be as clever as you portray them is quite another matter.

"That is not to suggest there are no outliers to the rule.

"Also, criminals usually do not admit to doing anything without a plea bargain or incentive.

"It was more your paralegal work and interest in how investigations work that made you stand out to me since we needed a skilled writer to maintain and fulfill our contracts.

"We have many high-profile clients, and we bring you on cases periodically because of your history with the legal system and your way of thinking."

All said and done, the food was delicious, and while not certified kosher, it seemed to complement the traditions in the style of preparation. That said, knowing what to make of the information I have learned is hard, and it certainly explained how we all came together like this as a team. Moreover, I wonder just a little bit how much more some of us know than we let on about things or how different our skills are in conveying what we know. PI Patrick Patterson could be a bit clumsy and lack common sense in how to get out of boxes, yet he seemed to do pretty well at getting us out of the last puzzle in the previous chapter. Then there is Cat Sleuth, who appears to have the least experience in solving crimes but has insight into the legal side. I understand the idea of having a team with comprehensive skills. Still, I have to wonder if he is here more to protect us legally than do the work of a Detective, seeing as how he seems to be interchanged with PI Patrick with some of the cases we worked on, even the less exciting ones. Either way, what we learned will mean for us in the future is still to be seen.

CHAPTER 6

HUNTING FOR HOLIDAYS

It is All Fun and Games

Some of you may be wondering about the point of that last chapter. It answers many questions regarding cases put to rest for now but raises many more. Little could I have guessed that after a period of almost nothing worth sharing here, another monumental case would present itself. Well, I suppose if it did not, there would be no book chronicling it because what would I even write if there was nothing to solve?

Fisherman's Warf in San Francisco, California, was our next destination. We arrived two days after Purim, March 14, 1998. Why does this matter? Well, it is customary for the Jewry of some observance to dress up as princes and princesses to collect money for charity, and adults, drink as much or more than people who celebrate St. Patrick's Day. Observation of it varies among Jewish people, but if they go to Temple, Synagogue, or Shule, they know of it. Few need much persuasion to party and be dumb in this country, so I am investigating. So far, the main suspect in the case was drunk off his bum and shot a few people when someone knocked on his door. If my sources are correct, the poor guy had PTSD from the Second great war and, with the lack of mental health services, was self-medicating to cope with the flashbacks. What triggered him, we do not yet know. Did he do it? We do not know. That is where this part of the story begins. I arrived at the scene where Leonard Rudder-Beaut, I keep almost saying "butt," was interviewing Henry Skins.

"I did not do it! I am a drunk, not a bloodthirsty murderer!"

"I understand, and I am not saying you had any involvement in this, just that a trail of evidence has led us here, and we want to know where you were on March 11-12, 1998."

"I was at home drinking myself to sleep the night of the 11th.

"Then, on the 12th, I assume I got a knock on my door.

"These two kids were dressed as a Prince and Princess. They had a donation box and asked me to contribute to a children's hospital.

"In my State of vulnerability, I listened to their story. One of the patients at the hospital was a child who would visit senior citizens at retirement homes and bring gift baskets for every holiday, but then one day, a car's failed brake systems put them in critical condition.

"As someone who relishes any joy I can still have, I donated a lot.

"I was involved in freeing Jewish people from the camps and seeing what looked like living zombies on the edge of death itself.

"There were many more atrocious things that I cannot mention without losing my head, of course."

"You sound like a pretty honorable man, but I will cut to the point.

"We found a couple of bodies in a nearby house with bullets that matched the kind of guns someone like you might have given your war experience."

Henry took a massive swig of alcohol and hunched over.

"I had some company over for a Pre-Saint Patrick's Day Reunion, and among them was a Thaddius Yu, Don Giovanni, and Axel Flask.

"Don Giovanni is not a mobster, just a weird naming coincidence.

"His parents were into theater despite rarely being able to afford it."

"And what did you all do when the party was on?"

"Well, we shared war stories over copious amounts of alcohol and danced to Irish music while feeling like complete trash in the best of ways."

"Did any of you do anything involving guns?"

"We showed off the war weapons we had brought back from the war and took turns firing them at some cans out back.

"I know how it sounds.

"We were not doing something brilliant."

While they were talking, I ventured to the backyard wall and noticed bullet holes in it in various places. I then peeked over the wall to see a somber silence beyond it. Hmm, how suspicious. If Henry is telling the truth, the rounds may have penetrated that house and possibly hit someone. This is at least a negligence suit both on the part of the guests and the owner.

"Uh, Mr. Rudder-Butt?"

"That's Rudder-Beaut! Freaking Americans..."

"Sorry Rudder-Beaut, you might want to look at this."

He came over, and I explained exactly what I found.

"Seems he is telling the truth.

"If he was shooting at cans, it is entirely possible some stray bullets could have wound up in a few houses.

"Though the targets appear to comply with basic gun safety.

"If that were so, it would be due to their inebriation that maybe one of them could have missed the targets in excitement."

"Yeah, but with so many of them involved, how will we know whose rounds did damage and who might have died?"

"That may be indeterminable.

However, if anyone did, they all are accessories, at minimum, to manslaughter for any who died.

"Key is proving they were all here."

He turned back to Henry, "Sorry about that, Mr. Skins.

"I am not going to lie to you.

"You know what liability you hold if your antics happened to accidentally or otherwise enter someone's home, right?"

He nodded sadly, holding his hands as if expecting us to cuff him, "Go ahead, whether I am free in my home or locked up, I will still be a prisoner of my mind and all I saw in the war.

"Besides, I may serve next to no time if I plead guilty."

"Unfortunately, it is not our authority to take you in.

"We just want answers."

"Fair, but as I said, I am pretty old now, about 75 last I checked.

"Even if they put me away for 15 years, it is doubtful I will live that much longer.

"I have no reason to deceive you."

"And nothing to lose with taking a few down with you?"

"I acted drunk and stupid.

"I am not some bloodthirsty murderer.

"Though I do not know if I can say the same for Thaddius.

"He seemed to enjoy knowing how many homes his inventions would break in building his war machines.

"Though he seemed otherwise lawful.

"Still, if anyone could have calculated the risk of killing someone with antics, it would have been him."

"Don, well, there is not much to say about him.

"He is a man of few words but commands the respect of just about anyone."

"Axel, I think he went on to found an underground band post-war.

"He lied about his age to enter the war in High School, so if I had to guess, he might be in his late 60s since we served around the same time.

"The youngest soldier to lie about their age was 14 at the time, and we kind of got in late being American."

"Interesting indeed. You have been most helpful in this."

We went to the house across from where they were shooting and found it not a pretty sight. Cops were surrounding the building paramedics had long left by this point.

"Ah, you are here.

"We have been expecting you."

"Oh?"

"Yeah, the details seem clear as day, but something is missing. Motive..."

"We just got done interviewing the homeowner behind this place.

"It seems he and some military buddies were shooting cans out back, and only one would have given no cares for who got hurt."

"Seems consistent with what we saw.

"The owners of this building were in pretty bad shape, and I doubt they will survive."

"So, what did you see of the bodies?"

"One had a bullet to the gut and through their back.

"The other had one through their leg and another right between the eyes."

I looked at the other side of the wall and the house.

"Weird, the bullet holes indicate the home's occupants either shot back at the guys in the backyard or whoever attacked them tried to make it look like they were shooting at the opposite home to theirs."

"If that is the case, the perp knew exactly what they were doing. We will have to question the survivors once discharged from the hospital." After collecting forensic evidence to bring back to the lab, Leonard Rudder-Beaut interviewed the one occupant who was still alive.

"It was not the house across from us nor ours.

"The assailant came in wearing a black cloak and what looked like ninja accessories.

"We tried to shoot it, but they were too fast.

"We heard the screams across the wall, and the assailant got away."

"That explains the strange weapons we found at your home and the gun holes in the wall."

"Yeah, hopefully, we did not hurt anyone on the other side."

It got more complicated when we thought it was such an open-and-shut case. A person in a ninja outfit, with people roaming about in costumes, would not seem that out of place. It seems only forensic analysis will have any hope of matching us to our perp.

Back in the lab, our scanners indicated the weapons had changed hands a few times before honing in on the last user.

Alan Saikumar Silverstein-Nakiah, or alias Assn the Assassin. He has a license to kill and is a bounty hunter. What could that family he attacked possibly have done for him to legally or not get shot? Though the police had apprehended him, he did not speak a word no matter what the police said. He did not even ask for a lawyer. It was a test of patience he was putting them through, by the sounds of it. Unfortunately, we still had to grant him a speedy trial, with or without his testimony. Discovery happened as expected, which will lead us to the next case.

Little did I know at the time that Silvester Shields got off the hook despite his conduct in the last chapter, but he had to take a deal to be Assn's defense attorney despite the fact we were all convinced he did it, so it would invariably be a loss right? Well, you will see.

Inside the court, Judge Incorrect was presiding as if predicting that he was notorious for letting the wrong judgments happen willfully. Silvester Shield's opponent was Daryl, Death Penalty.

"All parties have been sworn in.

"Now let us proceed with the case of Alan Saikumar Silverstein-Naikiah vs. The State of California.

"I will hear opening statements."

"The evidence collected will show that Mr. Silverstein-Nakiah used a party held by Mr. Skins as a convenient coverup for murder in cold blood.

"The killing was not sponsored or permitted by the State and broke a family not wanted by the law.

"Thus, their actions are strictly abusing their license to kill."

"And my evidence will show that it was reckless use of guns in the backyard of a San Francisco home that was to blame for their death of them.

"Alan was told to be in a specific place as part of a scouting mission to spy on people of interest.

"Consequently, my client found himself in a compromising situation where he would be accused of the murder of a family.

"The family of that owned backyard he had commandeered in the line of duty."

Silvester Shields looked professional, but I could tell he felt about as good about this as an anti-gun activist would feel being forced to be in a pro-gun campaign video. Daryl brought forth Exhibit A, the mysterious ninja weapons that should have made this an open-and-shut case. Exhibit B is the remnants we got back to the forensic lab. Exhibit C is the report based on everything found on the scene and analysis. Silvester Shields used the bullet holes in the fence as counter-evidence, the guns used at the party, and the interview with Mr. Skins about the circumstances surrounding the party.

I was called to the stand because my expert opinion was needed based on what I saw on the scene.

"I saw bullet holes coming from opposite sides of the fence.

"Based on the evidence, the deceased's family members and Henry Skins had guns.

"Given the trajectory of where the bullet holes were relative to the targets and deceased, it would appear the deceased family members saw Alan as a threat to their lives and acted to protect themselves.

"Then, unable to hit their target, a terrified Henry Skins could have awakened from a nap and returned fire.

"Despite the collateral damage and injuries done to the ones who survived the incident, it seems obvious the deceased did not die from gunshots, but instead whatever Alan did accidentally or otherwise.

"I am somewhat ashamed that Mr. Shields would take this side of the case knowing what facts are involved and the kinds of cases he worked on before."

"I have a family damn it! I have to feed them!"

"Order! You are on thin ice, Mr. Shields."

Sylvester nodded apologetically and let things resume.

"Now then, as I said, despite these coverup attempts by pointing out the holes, we also note how the gun range was set up.

"Despite the State of mind, the people were compliant with firearm safety as one might expect from someone who served in any branch of the armed forces.

"This is not to say their actions were not reckless for being under the influence.

"But instead, as it pertains to this case, it is unlikely they could have accidentally killed the family across the fence.

"Thank you, your honor."

"Very well, you may return to your seat."

I do as ordered by the judge and take my seat. There was no one to speak on behalf of Alan. And so came the verdict.

"We find the defendant Alan Saikumar Silverstein-Naikiah not guilty on all three counts of first-degree murder, Second Degree Murder, and Manslaughter."

The audience was shocked, as if someone guilty just went free, or people seldom get found not guilty around here. Either option does not bode well for justice. I went home, and despite Silvester Shields winning, he seemed to have sold his soul for money in defending this case to keep his position on the bar.

"The defendant in the above-entitled case has been found not guilty by a jury of his peers.

"He has thus been acquitted of any charges that would otherwise be rendered, and the case is dismissed.

"Have a wonderful weekend, everyone."

Outside I went back to my hotel as it was almost nighttime, and I did not feel like traveling home yet. I am so disgusted by what occurred today, but after you read the following few chapters, you will understand better why it all happened. Until then, I took a short break before the next groundbreaking case you will see in the next chapter.

CHAPTER 7

RIOT DEFY IT

Anarchy is in the Air

Not since the beating of an unarmed Black Wolf, Roderick Fang, in 1992 had the major cities of Los Angeles and San Francisco seen such an uprising. By this point, you may be wondering how this could be if, so far, my cases usually worked in favor of the furry involved or at least did not have them being put away for a time. While almost all my trials were handled well, that did not mean all were taken equally. Alan, aka Assn's, was just one example as he got off the hook in the last chapter, albeit not with a furry involved this time in his crimes.

Looking at the news, I could see cars flipped and people being run over with many wheeled devices, from motorcycles to stolen big rigs. The breaking news station had to work overtime to censor this carnage to be watchable for any decent person. There were even situations where news reporters were shot dead mid-report or run over. Thus, in hours, we could get no coverage on the ground, and all footage was captured via a news helicopter.

Good G-d, how was I expected to handle what would surely be a slew of forensic homicide cases that would surely arise from all this? Any worry about being a reliable person to speak in a court was quickly turned on its end when I saw some thugs outside my hotel room mow down security and begin destroying people's cars. It was then they aimed for mine. Not willing to take this lying down, I locked and loaded. Oh, the irony. I, too, might be a defendant in a murder case if I am not careful. Luckily, I have been supplied with non-lethal means of dispersing the masses.

I keep a riot kit and med kit in my lab coat which I never leave home without, and I wear civilian clothes underneath. Because I was a UP agent before Earth allowed us openly, both are highly portable, concealable, and versatile for the situation, much like multipurpose disaster bugout bags. I also have clearance to bring them into any venue by showing my badge.

I put on a gas mask and threw some smoke grenades toward my vehicle as they closed in on it. If they got their dirty hands on my vehicle, we could have a situation worse than a military invasion on our paws. Or did you forget how in Chapter 1, I mentioned my car though primitive-looking, is equipped with the means to leave this planet if there was no saving it? There is all I can say that there is more than escape tools. Amid the opening of the riot, I started my engine, put it into helicopter mode, and flew home. I did not want to do that, but the alternative would have left neither me to tell this story nor a world to do my work.

Once I was safely back over Torrance, I landed at Torrance Airport, on Sky Park Drive, a private airport for personal planes. Once on the ground, I showed my credentials to security personnel, then converted it back into a car and took to the road as I made my way home. Once home, I got an angry call from my boss.

"Lailah, you reckless fool.

"You should never have stayed in San Francisco after the trial, much less brought your convertible planetary escape vehicle.

"Do you know what could have happened if they had got ahold of your vehicle?

"No earth-made vehicle would be prepared to handle that, and it would cost us trillions to call down strikes from space to render it unusable and replace it."

"I know, Mr. Benson, and I quickly evacuated once I saw the blunder I had made."

"I will let you off with a warning this time, but if you come that close to losing your vehicle again, you are fired!"

He slammed the phone down, and I could tell it took all his restraint not to call me things that, under other circumstances, would be a civil case, to put it mildly. His reaction was justified; termination would be the least of my worries if a criminal got their hands on my vehicle.

I hope Adam and Neko are okay.

I got a video phone call from Neko as if my thought summoned him.

"Lailah, I have been forced to lock down my escape room.

"It is utter pandemonium."

A panda was running wild in the background of his home in Julian.

"I have taken shelter in Julian and am protecting my home with guns from any rioters that may have followed me.

"I presume Adam's situation is not much better."

"I surmised as much and do not expect any letters anytime soon.

"I guess the military and national guard will be dispersed to quell this, but I do not know how effective that will be.

"Whether they use lethal force and mow them down or let them live in pain, it does not bode well for regaining order."

"I know what you mean, but we can only wait and protect what is ours."

"Right. Well, I got to go.

"Rioters are at my door."

After what felt like forever and occasional clashes with unruly civilians, things eventually returned to normalcy. However, gang membership for furry and human gangs had increased significantly amid the civil unrest. That brings me to my case today.

Heaven's Demons attacked the Claws. In this case, the question is not whether or not they had a paw in the death, but which of them was defending themselves, or so I thought. As a Forensic Anthropologist, I should know it is never this easy by now.

For this case, I was taken to a place called Carson. It is a pretty low-key town with a university on the edge of it bordering Compton Long Beach and Harbor City. Over in those parts, one could expect to find neighborhoods of wolves and Foxes with some cats mixed between them. It was, however, not a place most humans wanted to be if they had other options. An effect of Furlining, they called it. Unless we had considerable skills and capability to live among humans, it was much less likely even back then to qualify for loans enabling the same wealth acquisition. Cat people, however, were seen as a token minority for all others to aspire to be, so they were not as discriminated against at first or not in the same way. It is why there is occasional resentment for them from their neighbors, but it pales in comparison to their hatred of humans. Even writing this is almost enough to make my blood boil. I digress. Because of such disparities, a unit like the one I am a part of is crucial to maintaining order and fairness.

I am going into the base of a group known as The Paws. As cute as their name is, they are a force to be reckoned with. Though not particularly out to commit crimes, humans frequently target them and naturally do what they must survive, or so I am told. As I mentioned, that does not make things any easier to solve.

"You are here.

"The boss is inside waiting."

I nod and enter my car, parked out of sight with alarms on so I could hear it if anyone pulled a fast one.

"Welcome. I have heard many things about you.

"You have a knack for finding the truth by any means necessary.

"Ah, where are my manners?

"I am Felix FeralPaw, leader of the Paws.

"I called you here because one of ours got his house full of holes, and no one but your division seems to give a rat posterior to find out who did it.

"Contrary to our organization's appearance, we are a civil rights group first and an avenging group second.

"The latter is always a last resort, for we banded together for safety.

"Unfortunately, the same cannot be said for the Claws, which we are often confused for if not for our differing wardrobes.

"They wear black and orange with scratch marks on their apparel, while we use pawprints and red and black.

"Watch out for them.

"They think they are the police for this town and are not concerned with who gets killed as long as they take their intended targets with them.

"Our last call from Linus Lynx said some humans were shooting at him.

"If anything is left of him, I fear the worst."

"So why did you ask me to come here?"

"These mean streets are no place for a Vixen like you."

"Spare me, your chivalry knight.

"I can handle myself fine."

"Okay, would it maybe make investigating a little easier if you have lookouts so you do not wind up a corpse on the scene of an investigation?"

"I suppose it would though then any cleanup would add another layer of sand to sift, that said it would be preferable to being the victim on the scene."

"Exactly, we are on your side.

"Justice cannot be done without irrefutable evidence of what has been done."

Reluctantly, but realizing the danger I am in the longer I linger here, I took them up on their offer. When I arrived, the ever-reliable P.I. Patrick Patterson was on the scene.

"Lailah, thank goodness you are here."

"What is the situation?"

"Well, it seems like the damage was gang motivated, but one thing does not add up."

"Oh?"

"The rounds found on the property that made the bullet holes appear to be a mismatch between it and the one we found on the body.

"While we know some guns are more capable, or interchanging rounds than others, the particular bullet used could only have come from an AK-47 while the others came from an Uzi."

"An Uzi cannot properly handle a Magnum and 7.62x51 NATO ammunition."

"Right, the rounds an Uzi uses are completely different than that of an AK-47 in every way."

"So, we conclude from this that either the person who did this is an avid user of a couple of different types of guns, or it was a multiple-man job."

"Correct, and to make matters more complicated, many people would have been motivated to do this because he is in a gang.

"Pretty sure no one will talk unless they value serving time in the gang."

"What is even odder is on the wall, and the bullets form the number 13.

"Most of the modern world thinks it is unlucky, but Jewish people consider it the opposite because G-d is believed to have 13 Attributes of Mercy.

"Either the killer has a sick sense of humor in that, or it is a weird coincidence."

"Weird thing to bring up here, but okay..."

"Well, I cannot shake how weird it was that we were trapped in a hotel and had to use clues like that to find our way out.

"The last case I was involved in happened on a lesser-known Jewish Holiday.

"There must be a connection here somewhere."

"It does seem a disturbing trend, but I do not think it has any deeper meaning.

"I mean, many people hate what they do not understand."

"Maybe... but it is not something I want to rule out completely.

"I mean, factions like them exist because of fear, but fear of what and what motive?"

"Wait, do you see that?"

I looked closer to see something I was not prepared to see. The one we thought was dead was still alive.

"What in the world is going on?

"Why are there bullets in my house?"

"That is what we would like to know.

"How could anyone have missed that many times?"

"Weird..."

I and PI Patrick searched further into the house to see the person owned an Uzi but not an AK-47.

"Do you remember anything about what you did today or the day prior?"

"Well, I was going about life as usual when I heard a bunch of popping.

"I was a little drunk off some Stolichnaya, and someone began firing these holes in my home, so I fired back."

"And then what happened?"

"I guess they drove off realizing they were outgunned quite literally."

On further investigation, it appeared the Uzi rounds had come from inside the house and the AK-47s from outside, given the marks they made entering and exiting.

"Do you have anyone who you can remember pissing off specifically?"

"No, I am a civil servant, so I mostly let bygones be bygones."

I thought for a moment.

"Okay, are you friends with any member of the claws?"

"Yeah, Clyde Claw"

"The leader of the Claws?"

"Yep, nice enough guy when you get passed his rough exterior and ambitions of a human-free world."

"A 'human-free world,' eh?

"Do you think he would have sent his goons to stage a fake killing attempt to frame a human gang?"

"Oh, I would not doubt it.

'The guy knows what he is doing.

"Gave me a special cocktail to help me sleep."

This is bad, really bad.

Either we must interrogate a gang kingpin or rely on the current evidence in front of us.

With no further questions, it was back to the lab with what evidence we found. The bullets and gun belonged to no identifiable gang member except the Uzi, which we confirmed belonged to Linus Lynx.

What could it all mean?

And whatever happened to the lost suspect from Chapter 2?

Could he be engineering these guns and giving them to those who commit unsolved crimes?

None of this makes any sense.

Moreover, how is that guy still alive?

Indeed, he should have been hit at least once.

That is, given the position we found him and where the bullets went in and out.

Unless... someone moved the body, if there was one or both, willingly made bullet holes there as a distraction to keep us off their trail.

And then I spotted a card for Hammer and tails construction company. Somehow it had been slipped into my pockets when I was talking to the presumed dead one.

But they are still in jail.

Unless we did not find all of their members.

That would not be a massive surprise if they had a high turnover rate.

But why would they care about any of this?

They don't. It is so apparent some gang that hates Furries has sprung up under their trademark to taunt them.

This has become too much to process alone.

"Lailah!"

Suddenly I came back to the moment.

"Yes!"

"We found it!"

"Found what?"

"We interviewed the leader of the Claws, and he was all too happy to point us to the culprit."

"And you trust him...Why?"

"Because all the evidence we found thus far points to them."

"I do not believe it, but I will humor your lead if only to unravel the web of lies."

Following the lead, we were taken to a dumpy-looking building in the impoverished area known as skid row. Trash was everywhere, and people experiencing homelessness huddled together across the street. Investigating the waste bins here would be dangerous as there could be discarded needles. Due to defunding of mental institutions, these poor souls had nowhere to go to get help for addiction or mental health concerns that led to it. Meanwhile, politics would rather see them as a failure than the potential they once had before it all went to hell. The building itself appeared to be a soup kitchen of sorts. Inside there was a volunteer lead.

"Lost your home too?"

"No, we were told you might know of a Linus Lynx?"

"That drunken civil servant?

"Yeah, if I had a nickel for every time he drunkenly wound up here, I would be rich.

"Most ruffian types consider this neutral drug-dealing territory, make no noise, and all is fair.

"Even some hardened criminals never want to come down these parts.

"Anyways, what did you want to know?"

"Well, we found bullet holes in his house that were his, and some we confirmed were not.

"We suspect the leader of Claws might have staged this based on what he told us and the fact he was alive."

"I wouldn't believe a drunk, honestly.

"But short of dumb luck, a more likely scenario, he thought he heard gunshots and returned fire.

"Then whoever fired back did so to stay alive irrespective of who it was and fled the scene when that option was not viable.

"Regardless, without a body, it is less a murder mystery and more a vandalism and maybe assault investigation."

"Yeah, but you do not think with him being friends with a gang, they would not have hidden the body of whoever they killed and planted him there?"

"Always possible, but the closest body of water to them that one might swim nearby would be the Dominguez Channel or Compton Creek.

"Which was chosen would likely depend on where the shootout occurred, but since you were investigating Carson, I think you know which is more probable."

With this new information, I sent rescue crews to find the body. If dumped in the Dominguez Channel, they would likely be in Los Angeles or Long Beach Harbor by now. Whether by luck or a good lead, the body was recovered, albeit eaten by fish to some extent at Terminal Island. The victim was none other than Nigel Nightingale. Upon picking inside his pockets, we found a Hammer and Tails construction company card. Upon submission of the body to the forensics labs, we found a barrage of Uzi rounds on his body. Whether accidental or otherwise, Linus Lynx did the deed, so he was naturally questioned and soon put on trial. What remains unsolved, though, is who engineered weapons that were not registered in any database. It seems clear someone knows how to acquire the necessary parts to do it and assemble them, but who? I must put that question aside as I prepare to provide the Jury with my expert opinion. Only it will not be as open and shut as previous cases if I learned nothing else from Lily Lockup. Any lawyer knows being drunk and stupid is not a valid defense, but was Mr. Nightingale an innocent bystander or a real threat to him? We cannot precisely question the dead.

And so, the day of the trial began. As expected, it did not look good for him as Linus had not exercised the right to have an attorney present during questioning; however, considering how easily Assn got off, it might not be so sure. Judge Mathias Monsoon presided, and for once, we get a judge without a weirdly specific first and last name.

"We now gather to hear the case of Linus Lynx vs. The State of California."

Prosecutor Orvin Plaid made his opening statement.

"The evidence meticulously collected here will show that Linus Lynx did, in fact, murder Nigel Nightingale not in self-defense, but because of his self-inflicted impaired judgment."

Defense Attorney Cait Smith then presented his opening statement when appropriate, "And I say the evidence will show the defendant Linus Lynx acted in self-defense and no reasonable person would have thought themselves safe in what transpired."

"Excellent let's look at the evidence."

"Exhibit A high-quality photograph of the bullet holes on both sides of the house.

"Exhibit B the guns used in staging a murder.

"Exhibit C The Forensic File and autopsy reports of the Deceased.

"Exhibit D the recorded police confession."

The prosecutor looked smug.

"You see, one gun that made those holes is confirmed to belong to the defendant while the other one, while unregistered more than likely belonged to one of the Claws or Paws members.

"It would be perfect; too, the Claws want a human-free world.

"So, what better way to get the holdout paws to join them in their crimes than stage a death of one of their own!

"However, Mr. Nightingale was in the area at the time of the staged murder.

"The Claws could not let anyone know what they were up to, so they had to silence him permanently.

"They even sent him down the river to the ocean to hide the deed."

Monsoon seemed intrigued, "And the defense?"

Cait Smith shook his head disapprovingly, "The theory the prosecution is riding on is a bunch of Malarky.

"My client is of an upstanding civil rights group out to do something about the racism humans have shown various races over the years.

"Racism spurred them into forming gangs to protect themselves.

"The fact the other gun is unregistered means it could belong to anyone.

"My mom could own that gun for all anyone knows, and she is anti-gun."

The prosecutor interjected, "Did you hear that, Jury?

"The defense attorney just confessed to his mom owning the other gun, and dare I mention he is not human either?"

"See? This flagrant disregard for civil rights got us into this mess!"

"Order Bast, damn it!" The Judge banged his gavel angrily.

"This has nothing to do with Cait Smith's race.

"The question we want to be answered is whether or not their client did the deed!"

Whew, did Mr. Monsoon live up to his name? He is a storm of anger when people act out of line.

"What I was trying to get at in my statement is that without an identified owner, the gun could have belonged to the deceased one today.

"If that were true, my client could have acted in self-defense."

Judge Monsoon seemed intrigued by the theory.

Prosecutor Orvan Plaid pointed to Exhibit C, "That is where the autopsy report comes in, your honor.

"As you will notice from the conclusions of this carefully written document, the bullets that went into the victim were from the registered Uzi."

Defense Attorney Cait Smith countered, "That may be so, but it says nothing about the deceased's actions before their life was cut short or motive.

"Seeing as we still have an ownerless weapon, we cannot conclusively confirm nor deny that another was not involved.

"We cannot prove the one who died did not threaten my client.

"A reasonable person, if faced with the barrel of another gun, would have no recourse but to run or fight.

"My client did what made the most sense to preserve their life.

"Might I also add the deceased had a card belonging to the Hammer and Tails Construction Company when he was found, per the forensic reports?

"Whoever owned the unidentified weapon was part of some terrorist organization against Furries.

"And where did the report say they found that calling card?

"Why it was on the body of Mr. Nightingale.

"Considering what horrors befell humans in 1994 and the atrocities towards the one furry survivor, it would be akin to having a business card with a swastika in the eyes of Furries.

"Thus, sober or not, my client would have taken it and them having a firearm as a potential threat."

The prosecutor scoffed, "Akin to a swastika?

"You realize that is an offensive diminishment of a historical genocide, right?"

"Okay, perhaps not that extreme a comparison point.

"However, given what it means in the context of events in 1994, it is understood to be a new hate symbol.

"People using it not only dump on the memory of the families who died in the tragedy but also represent the mistrust it sowed towards the furry races.

"A furry was the only survivor and scapegoat for the whole thing despite what the evidence demonstrated.

"Need I remind you this conspiracy had a Lawyer put away for a long time almost a year ago?

"The one surviving cat's family was murdered over it.

"While it may not yet have the same historical significance, the cases were high profile enough that unless you lived under a rock or in some other State, you could not walk a block without hearing about it.

"The word would spread either by passers-by or news outlets.

"Therefore, a reasonable person, even without the hate card, would see one as a threat had they pulled a gun on them.

"The prosecution has failed beyond a reasonable doubt to prove that my client did not act out of self-preservation.

"Therefore, I ask that the Jury consider that in their deliberation."

The prosecutor smirked briefly, "What about the police tape?"

We listened to the police tape where in the interrogation room, the defendant was heard saying he shot the guy but would be killed if he didn't. The police reminded him he could go with minimal penalties if he just came clean about his real intent. The tape indicated 10 hours or so had passed.

Mr. Lynx said on the tape, "Okay, I did it.

"I shot him in cold blood.

I knew we could better protect furry kind by uniting the forces together.

"Now, can I please change out of these piss-stained clothes?

"You all would not let me use the bathroom this whole time."

The defense looked even more confident than before, "My client told what I presume is the truth the first time.

"However, by the admission of your police tape and my client, you interrogated him for 10 hours without a bathroom break.

"He pissed himself and would have said anything not to have to wallow in it any longer.

"This confession was under duress, and thus I motion to throw it out."

Judge Monsoon, "Motion sustained."

Prosecutor Orvan Plaid retorted, "Despite the lack of efficacy of the last bit of evidence, I call into question why they would dump the body down the river if it were self-defense?"

Defense Attorney Cait Smith said, "We do not know who dumped the body.

"Any fingerprints would have been washed away in the ocean."

Prosecutor Orvan Plaid nodded, "I call Lailah Yarakah to the stand to give her expert opinion."

Finally, I took the stand. I felt uneasy as I wanted to be fair, but in a racially charged case like this, I am not scoring points with whoever's side loses, even if I am impartial.

"Yes, as you all have seen of the autopsy reports, we confirmed whose bullets went in the body.

"We still do not have an owner of the second gun.

"The card in their pocket suggests they may have born some resentment, but for who is unclear.

"He may have been a human despite his last name, but it is unclear if he carried that card out of hatred for humanity.

"We also cannot confirm or deny if a gang is using it in the way Mr. Smith suggested.

"It is too new for the Southern Poverty Law Center or the Furry Law Center to have a conclusion.

"Nevertheless, it does raise questions about what sort of person would be carrying that, not to mention a military-grade weapon where it could be found.

"And what do you suppose is the likelihood Mr. Nightingale could have owned such a thing, much less have acquired it?

"Nothing in the criminal records database suggests he would have done anything to anyone.

"However, he did have a parent who served in the armed forces, which might explain how he could have acquired that gun.

"But they would have had to register it before leaving the base.

"Given an investigation where a gun was unregistered before and a missing defendant, it is possible.

"If he knew how to build a weapon, he could have assembled the parts and never registered it.

"Otherwise, nothing we found can decisively prove that Mr. Nightingale did or did not have that weapon, regardless of how they may have acquired it the day he died.

"I find it a little suspicious that this guy was friends with the head of Claws despite being part of a more pacifist group.

"One aims to change the world through nonviolence but doing what they must survive.

"Nevertheless, in the same way, having friends of a race does not mean you are not racist, neither does friendship with a gang member means you are necessarily a criminal."

"That will do, Lailah. Thank you."

The Judge seemed slightly impatient at how nowhere this was getting, "If there are no more witnesses, I suggest we move to conclude arguments and then have the Jury reach a verdict."

Prosecutor Orvan Plaid concluded, "In summation, what we have here is a human who this Lynx felled.

"The defense has not attempted to disprove the fact, but the motive seems clear.

"Based on his gang affiliation and the fact he was drunk that day, he was in no position to make a life-or-death decision, much less be anywhere near a gun."

Defense Attorney Cait Smith concluded, "And I say, his drunken state is irrelevant as we cannot determine whether Mr. Nightingale credibly threatened him.

"We do not conclusively know who owned the second gun found on the scene, and he had the sense to act lawfully to register the weapon he used.

"It is safe to assume he acted in self-defense and should be found not guilty of all murder charges and manslaughter ones."

The Jury went back to discuss the facts of the case and came back.

"Has the Jury reached a verdict?"

"Not guilty of all counts of murder and manslaughter because of self-defense and insufficient evidence that someone else was not involved or the victim did not threaten him."

"Mr. Lynx is free to go.

"While beyond the scope of this case, I should suggest the ones who refused the defendant a bathroom break be subject to potential penalties for their actions.

"As for this case, the court is adjourned."

He banged his gavel.

And that was how the case ended. Although the Judge was human and ruled in favor of the Jury, hate crimes increased. Furry homes soon found the hammer and nails construction company logo carved into exterior walls and mowed into their lawns, among other similar things Adam faced in Chapter 1. Despite my sending letters after this case, he has not since responded. I did not find it unusual, though, as he would naturally get busy with schoolwork and life as he ages.

CHAPTER 8

THE DOOK OF EARL

The Mischievous Ruler of the Underground

I came home to find even my home was vandalized. It seems even my presence has nearly worn out its welcome here. Just as, well, I cannot control others, just me. But they need to work on their artistic skill. That caricature of my face on my garage looks like something a kindergarten kid would draw. Cute, out of context, but pathetic when used insultingly.

I digress. I can never truly have a vacation from the political landscape quickly taking hold across this land. I wish we could be more like Egypt; they love and worship Furries like us. Speaking of which, it seems humans aren't the only ones stirring the pot, or so I am told. I am above the level where I investigate petty crimes, and I have to wonder how much shit people who do take for their role. As I began tending my backyard, a ferret scampered by, making chitters that humans call "dooking." Cute little thing it is, but what could it be doing here, of all places?

It dropped a letter at my paws and hopped the fence. Well, that is one way to deliver the mail, but what could it be? I opened the letter to find it was an invitation to a party to celebrate the Dook of Earl. Is this some prank or executed pun on some 1960s doo-wop song? The address seems legit, though. It was one of the numbered addresses on Earl St. in Torrance with the zip code 90503. I followed it to the address and saw what seemed like a reasonably average house, but there was a party going on, and sure enough, this "Dook of Earl" was wearing a crown and making excited ferret sounds. As I made my way over, I saw many pieces of shiny jewelry and ornaments, quite becoming one to hold such a title. Then I began to question why I was here and its implications.

What looked to be the mysterious ferret's mother appeared.

"Ah, hello there, young fox. I presume you are here to see Hunter."

"You mean the one that gave me this letter?"

"The same, the name is Ruby Furlington, and the quiet man next to me is Copper Furlington.

"Incidentally, Hunter hasn't swiped anything from you, right?"

I checked my pockets to notice all seemed accounted for on my person.

"Not that I can tell."

"Ah, good. We have been trying to help Hunter through his impulses, one of which seems to be collecting shiny objects.

"We do not know where he gets them from, but he insists people give him things for being adorable.

"I always told him one day he would get himself stomped if he ever got caught stealing."

"Well, petty theft is outside my jurisdiction as I handle more cases of people being 'stomped' to death.

"Though it grossly oversimplifies the severity and complexity of cases I have got of late."

"Ah yes, a Forensic Anthropologist, I presume?"

"Yeah, but like oddly specific guess on your part as there are many dimensions to forensics."

"Well, because your work requires you to give an expert opinion, surely you know you aren't a secret agent, right?"

"Yeah, but who has time to keep up with the many cases I am involved in?"

"You may not know it, but you are a popular figure.

"Praised by that which has fluff while scorned by that which lacks it to some degree."

"That explains the vandalism to my house.

"Anyways, what makes you think your son is a thief?"

"Well, with all the hate towards us furred types lately, I worry Hunter will one day find himself in a gang for protection.

"Or worse, get himself killed due to stereotypes about our species that involve stealing.

"It is not that we think he does, but that it is a prevailing notion that has been used to justify incarceration and even stomping us half to death in years past."

"Yeah, seems fertile ground for potential criminality with those risks present.

"So, what is this party about anyway?"

"Well, it is Hunter's Birthday, so he decided on a royalty theme for it hence all those flashy jewels you see about the place."

"Right, not to offend, but that is not how one spells Duke as in the royalty."

"That is the pun.

"We used to call him our little Dooker, and he lives on Earl Street, so we dubbed him 'The Dook of Earl,' not to be confused with that 1960s song."

"Makes sense to me, so did he give these out to the whole city of Torrance?

"Seems random, and I get one when I never even met."

"Well, he is your biggest fan.

"When he sees you go up and give your opinion, which often exonerates the furry suspects and gets the humans put away, he makes the cutest sounds of joy."

"You let him watch the trials on T.V.?"

"Yeah, he enjoys them a lot, and we would love nothing more than to see him happy.

"Would you like some cake?"

"Uh, sure, I suppose.

"Not like I am watching my figure for anyone."

I laughed somewhat awkwardly, having revealed a little nugget of truth there. As a rule, I do not see myself as having time for relationships and family. In a sense, the various races of Furries are my family, and I owe it to them that justice is done when they are wronged. Even when I try to make time for vacation, you all see it becomes an investigation of its own. Frankly, I start to question my mental state amid those facts. So, even having this unexpected party invitation is a breath of fresh air. As I devour my cake and try to relax for once, I feel uneasy in my gut that something awful will happen, but I cannot place where or when exactly. It is a feeling I often experience, but it is more intense now, like someone was out to get me.

"Lailah, come watch me break the Pinata!"

"Okay, now."

I put on my best smile, as I cannot show too much concern around children. Sure enough, Hunter beat the object with the enthusiasm and bravery one might expect of one so young. And we all got some candy. I will need extra meditation to sleep tonight and an effective workout to remain in shape. If that close theft of my vehicle a couple of chapters ago was any indication, I am not immune from being targeted.

Then came the presents and I had one for him too. While something of a hard one inside, I still keep various toys appropriate for multiple ages handy. It goes back to my time as a Nurse at this story's beginning before my role as a Forensic Anthropologist, and I was very popular with child patients for it. I watched happily as he violently tore through the present wrapping to discover what else but a glow-in-the-dark teddy bear. As nightfall approached, I explained that it glows in the dark, so as the party came to a close, he hugged me as I left into the night.

"That plush toy should help you sleep better at night, knowing no bad people will come in without risking being seen."

"Thank you, Grandma Lailah."

No, I did not age a lot since the last chapter. It is just for someone that young. I would seem proportionately older and unimaginable.

Though I should remind you, I was alive through the 1960s and look like one in my 20s. But then, is he a kid, or was this all a setup? Ah, paranoia, I hate you. I drove off as Hunter stood there waving goodbye. You might think this is where the chapter ends, but there is more. Back to work the next day, I discovered their neighborhood was targeted at night. My boss was distraught. Am I cursed? Is everyone I try to connect with destined to meet a horrible fate?

"Lailah, this is bad.

"The family you visited; it seems someone abducted their child.

"An Amber alert has been issued, but it is uncertain whether we will find him.

"I do not usually send a forensics specialist for this, but they were a close friend of mine.

"You are the best we have.

"If you can find any clues in the house that might help us track them, we can get this done."

"Say no more.

"If I learned anything from previous cases, it is never just a missing person or what have you.

"There is something bigger at work.

"I can feel it."

"Glad you are on board, but I wouldn't jump to that conclusion.

"There are many cases we usually do not assign you because they are beneath your skill set."

I nodded, took off with my car, parked it near the house, and was greeted by two crying parents.

"Our son, someone has our son!"

"That is why I am here.

"I usually do not do these kinds of cases, but I will make the exception.

"I need to inspect the home for clues if we hope to find him."

They nod understanding, and I check downstairs, finding it seemingly untouched by a break-in. Then I went up the stairs, where I found more promising signs. Plush toys were strewn about the kid's room, and blood was on the carpet. It was as if the kid had tried to escape by biting whoever came in and got knocked unconscious. Upon further inspection, I also noted furry footprints that were too big to be Hunter's.

Impossible. There is no way one of our own would do this!

Not of their own volition...wait, there are shoe prints under the paw prints. Hmmm...

I looked at the bed and saw the sheets in tatters and a broken window. Upon going next to the broken window, I saw a hidden underground tunnel that led through the walls and under the floorboards. Weird... following the tunnel and trail of blood, it seemed to go on for miles and miles. My GPS device said I was heading down the street, and after significant paces were made, it appeared to lead towards Northern California. A couple of split paths led west and east, presumably to Catalina Island and Nevada in the east and San Francisco north, the route into Mexico south.

This is not good. If the suspect crosses the border, I must get an extradition order to pursue this further.

After traveling several miles, exhausting most of my energy following the footprints, they led to a cellar like the underground railroad would have used as a rest stop house on the way to Canada. I never thought my knowledge of history would have come in handy here. I popped up to see the tracks leading up to the bedroom. When I went up the stairs, I saw the Dook of Earl trembling there like he had seen a ghost.

"What happened here?"

"B-Behind you!"

I looked behind and instinctively grabbed the stranger coming up behind me, slammed him down, and disarmed him. It was, to my shock, a fox man. While pinning him down, I began interrogating him.

"What in Bast's name are you doing with this child?

"More importantly, why did you come behind me like that?"

After a groan from being disarmed skillfully, he spoke, "Things are not as they seem, I am Proctavius Lee Foxx, but you can refer to me as Proxy Foxy.

"To keep the explanation brief, I have intel that leads me to believe there is a pattern where every time you make a friend, they will invariably have the worst happen to them."

"And the blood on the carpet?"

He pulled back a patch of fur to show he had been shot in the arm.

"I took this bullet for the kid.

"Someone shot me while trying to kidnap him in his sleep, or did you not see the bullet hole in the wall or window?

"He was a lousy shot, but I surmise the ninja garb was a disguise."

"So, the violence has made its way to Torrance?"

"Yeah, no place is 100% safe."

Practically on my last nerve, now my body twitched in disbelief.

"'It is a simple rescue mission,' they said, 'do not get over-excited about it,' they said."

"I know this is a lot to take.

"I would be just as well whatever you call that emotion you are experiencing."

"It is a lot of emotions right now."

"Well, why would they send a forensic anthropologist to solve this case?"

"My boss, Bill Benson, said it was his close personal friend."

"Hmm, considering he and I once worked together, I should see why, as friendships, among other forms of relationships with people in this business, are dangerous to all we hold dear."

"You worked with him?"

"Yeah, they called him 'Bullet Breaker Bill Benson.'"

"Do tell."

"He was fearless both in the army and the police force, I am told.

"'Would take a bullet for us any day of the week and spit it out his maw.'"

"Course, back then, we had to have human disguises to live amongst them, as you may recall."

"The UP had reservations about us joining the battle; if any of us died, it could reveal our existence before they were ready.

"So, we compromised and took on more civilian-like roles such as medics and kitchen staff.

"We also had strict orders not to use our advanced techs for any of those purposes.

"Nevertheless, it did not stop humans from raiding encampments, so if they gave us guns, we could use those, but otherwise, no.

"If anyone of us died, UP operatives would dispose of them accordingly and wipe the memories of anyone who may have seen them.

"My job involved overseeing the creation of what humans would later call the internet.

"A more primitive form of communication most other planet's inhabitants use to stay in touch everywhere.

"Because of that, I had insight into how it worked and could monitor its use."

"Sounds interesting, so how did you come to know him?"

"While helping develop what humans called the technology of tomorrow, I chanced to meet him by invitation of Thaddius Yu and Don Giovanni.

"On breaks from work, we would all go to the same drinking spot, 'The Tired Tinkerer Tavern,' and eventually, we broke the ice.

"While we were drinking, Thaddius spoke of a Soldier who was becoming the talk of the front lines for whom he was building weapons and machines.

"Curious, and as a dare, we decided to let him join us one night.

"So, we did and exchanged our stories of things we had seen and discovered that he was not just a mindless soldier drone and suggested after the War he might become a police officer and maybe a forensic detective.

"He followed our advice and took it further by forming an agency.

"Impressed by his go-getter spirit and love of justice, I recommended to the UP Council that we do some tests on him to extend his life expectancy.

"We have had furry beings undergo age regression via fountain of youth and saw what side effects it had on their children, but we did not ever try it on humans.

"It will probably be some time before we see how effective it is at extending life, but we can at least confirm it made him look younger and probably feel as energetic as he looks."

"Yeah, Bill told me about the antiaging.

"Anyways, if The Furlington Family is such a huge ally of his, why did he not investigate this case?"

"Simple, he would have had too much bias knowing them far longer than you. It would compromise the investigation's integrity, and knowing them for a day is not knowing them."

"Wait, how did you know?"

"That car of yours, we have it on our radar and always know what you are up to. So, keep your muzzle clean."

"That explains how he knew it was almost stolen."

"Mhm, he thinks highly of you; otherwise, he would have fired you after that one."

"So, does he know now that you have the boy since I am here?"

"Yes, I reported to him we have the kid."

"Then what was the use of sending me?"

"I am search and rescue. You have the background to find the Mother Hubbards that tried to abduct this one."

"I guess..."

"Oh, come now, you helped bring to justice one of the most notorious syndicates in the world right now."

"You mean those scammy contractors, the Hammer & Tails?"

"The very same.

"You do not seriously believe a company as awful as them did not have some serious backing to have survived past their first year with their substandard craftsmanship, did you?"

"No, but I never figured it was much more than just working for the lower bidders and government."

"Well, it is.

"I do not know how yet, but I have concluded whoever is allowing these things to happen is someone with intimate knowledge of police procedure. But who?"

"I just do not know.

"With all the insanity lately, I hardly know what to make of it.

"Just when I think the answer is there, I attribute it to paranoia."

"You would be crazy not to, but something tells me you are closer to the truth than you know."

"I would imagine as much if people like you try to ambush me like that."

"I am the least of your worries."

"So, you say, I found both your paw prints and a human shoe print.

"Care to explain?"

"Well, while doing some observation work, I saw a suspicious figure dressed in ninja garbs approaching the building.

"He went inside, and I followed him.

"When he grabbed the kid, I tried to take him down as I would have you."

"Why did you try to take me down?"

"Because I thought you were the one who meant harm to this one.

"As I had told the boy to wait where he did, expecting the intruder to have followed me, that is, if he was really after the kid."

"So, I got mixed in your stupidly executed plan?"

"Pretty much.

"Now, can you get off me already?

"It is hard to breathe."

"Fine, but any sudden moves and I fully intend to incapacitate you properly."

"Noted..."

I got off him, and he brushed himself off as I pondered the plausibility of what he said. Wasting little time, Proxy pulled out his med kit and began removing the bullet from his arm with a scalpel. He dumped ointment and rubbed alcohol on it, wincing and letting out stifled screams as he bit into a block and began needling and threading the wound with a one-handed medical sewing brush. A medical sewing brush is a device that looks like a hairbrush but is like a flashlight. A button activates it, and you wave it in your desired direction. In this case, one would press and hold a button and move it along to sew up their wound. Such a device has been a lifesaver on planets with less advanced technological infrastructure, like Earth. All that explanation aside, I could not shake the thought of what I had seen and what it meant for us.

Those footprints, the blood, the situation we are in.

Is it my place to question the ethics or report what amounts to voluntary abduction as far as the legal system knows?

Or do I go along with it knowing justice has been unreliable lately?

Loathe, I am to get my paws dirty, but if it prevents a tragedy, I suppose my moral compass compels me to let it be.

But what will I tell my boss?

"I have a feeling I know who came after this guy.

"Recently, a killer was released by self-defense plea who fit your description."

"Who?"

"Alan Saikumar Silverstein-Nakiah or Assn the Assassin as he calls himself."

"I know who you mean, but that would be too obvious."

"Only one way to find out.

"I thought ahead and returned the scene samples to the lab."

"Good."

Little could I have guessed where the lab results pointed next.

"Las Vegas?"

Bill Benson looked over my shoulder.

"Ooo, what a fun place to be.

"Just do not gamble away all your money there."

I narrowed my eyes at him.

"Relax, I know you are better than that."

"Sure... but after the last case I worked on properly and now an attempted murder abduction, I have to question the company you keep, sir."

"In the armed forces, loyalty is first, regardless of type or branch.

"It can be a double-edged sword if one is up to no good.

"I am beginning to get suspicious of some of my old connections, but without a case and warrant to search, there is only so much we can legally do.

"Even if we are not police, we must obey trespass and search and seizure laws."

"I just do not know what to make of it.

"Proctavius or Proxy tried to attack me until I restrained him, and he supposedly knew where to be to protect the kid.

"Does any of that not seem suspicious?"

"Maybe a little, but I trust he can track most any threat to people of interest to me if he suspects something."

"If you say so."

With little else to do and a conversation likely to get nowhere with the boss, I resumed course and relayed the info to the team, and Cat Sleuth took to investigating alongside PI Patrick.

This was their report and corresponding audio logs:

Interview with Don Giovanni

The forensics analysis Lailah provided us led us to Las Vegas, specifically to the Cash Drop Casino, which, as its name suggests, was the sort of place you drop your cash, and your visit will be unforgettable. More accurately, it was the Las Vegas Strip in Paradise City, Nevada. Light shows on the hour, and sleazy people with cards tried convincing you to attend their club. Independent artists and musicians tried to solicit you to buy their merch. In a way not that different from the Hollywood Walk of Fame area, where people pose for photos for tips or Venice Beach or Santa Monica Beach. Don Giovanni owned the Casino and inherited it from his father, Ron Giovanni.

This was the exchange between us.

"Ey, how ya doing today?"

"Good. We thank you for your time, Mr. Giovanni.

"As we know, ya got a business to run here."

"This is what it is.

"I got no affiliation with anyone terrible.

"I served my time in the forces and bought a casino from some interesting people."

"Yeah, about that.

"We have reason to believe a kid who was family friends with Bill Benson may have been involved in some attempted attack, maybe?"

"Oh yeah, I knew him.

"He and Thaddius Yu were decent buds.

"Unfortunately, they both got in and out with a not-so-good crowd."

"Oh, is that so?"

"They call themselves the 'Heavens Demons.'

"Thaddius Yu was once one of them, and now he is hiding from them.

"I did not fancy joining clubs.

"I preferred to do things my way, which was reflected in my rank in the Second Great War."

"Tell me more."

"Well, there is not much to tell.

"Fortunately, I had the mental acuity to be trusted to work on the Manhattan Project behind the scenes, Engineering the Atomic Bombs Dropped on Hiroshima and Nagasaki.

"I oversaw it to completion.

"I guess I am not a total loner, but I had nothing to prove with such achievement.

"Nothing could have prepared me for the ethical ramifications of what I helped create, so I quit the military the first chance I got and did not feel the same camaraderie the others did.

"It is different when you are on the front lines trusting each other with your life or working in the same department.

"Still, they urged me to attend a reunion a few months ago, and I took them up.

"Then Henry got mixed into a conspiracy around the wrongful death of his neighbors.

"I swear it would have only been a matter of time before I shared his fate in that way.

"With that in mind, I will leave this place in the capable hands of my successors, Vincent Giovanni and Vanessa Giovanni.

"Then they will pass it on to their children when they are my age or pass on.

"They run it all now, and I provide advice and mentorship through various occurrences.

"This is why I found time to talk to you today."

"That is all well and good, but I think we got a bit off track.

"A kid was almost killed, and the evidence left behind led us here.

"Is anyone on a banned patron list who you feel had it in them to do this?"

"Well, there was one person here some time ago.

"Guy looked pretty shaken up, like more than the usual drug addict or alcoholic."

"Go on."

"I supported my grown-up kids because they immediately sensed something was up.

"I caught a strange-looking calling card when he presented his I.D. and payment cards.

"It had a logo with a Hammer and multiple animal tails."

"Weird we just put away such an organization with our findings back in 1994."

"Well, like the Nazi party before them, there would surely be a Neo Faction to follow given the hate, so it may well be that a group appropriated it to mean something."

"Are they still checked into your casino?"

"They never completed checkout.

"They were assigned to room 411."

"Thank you. We will inform the local authorities and prepare a trap for them."

"Sounds serious but do what you must. I got a bad feeling about this."

The trap set Paradise P.D. stopped the man on his return trip to his hotel room, and we began the interview with Carlos Diablo.

"Who are you?"

"I am Carlos Diablo of the Tool Tails."

"Why do you carry the card with the Hammer and Tails Construction Company Logo?"

"Because our Business feels a great sympathy for them.

"They did what they were paid to do.

"They warned their clients when buildings were not to code but had sunk too much into their projects.

"Refusing payment was off the table for them."

"So, you are contractors?"

"Yes, one of those awful gang members killed one of our best when he was just passing through to do a job."

"What kind of job?"

"The Heavens Demons wanted us to renovate their newest compound.

"One that just so happened to be on the border between their turf and that of the Claws.

"We did not think, being non-gang members, that we would have problems going through various territories as a third party, but we were dead wrong.

"I was not there when our Project Leader met his end, but I know he did not have a weapon on him that day."

"So, you are suggesting one was planted on him?"

"Yeah, but by who I could never know."

"Very peculiar indeed.

"So that explains your calling card and all.

"But why were you here in Las Vegas, and why did you look like you had just killed someone when you checked in here?"

"The Heaven's Demons told me they suspected someone affiliated with the Claws was operating out of Torrance and wanted me to investigate it.

"They promised me not just money but a place within their ranks so I would be protected and not end up like Mr. Nightingale.

"Per their request, I researched the man in question.

"When they caught wind of the one they suspected had a kid and was mutual friends with Lailah, who was blamed for a murderer of one of my crew going free, there was a change in plans.

"They were going to use the information I gave them to plan an attack on the gang member but instead saw more gain in taking the next of kin for ransom.

"They would ask for a sum the family could never pay and then kill the child whether or not anyone else helped them get the cash to avenge my fellow contractor's death and get back at the gang.

"As a bonus, they would also emotionally damage Lailah, who they blamed for the Paws member going free despite evidence suggesting he killed the man whether in self-defense or not."

"That is insane. One thing to try and kill a rival gang member but another to abduct and kill a child."

"I thought so too.

"I even asked them what would happen should I not want to do this, and they went into gut-wrenching detail of the slow and painful way they would do me in if I chickened out or refused to take the mission.

"I have the whole conversation of what was asked of me recorded to ensure I knew exactly what I was made to do and what would happen if I did not.

"Luckily, he seemed not to notice I had an audio recording device built into my hard hat, or he was sure I would not turn it in knowing the severe bodily harm he promised if I went back on the contract.

"Even still, I think jail time for kidnapping and assault while having connections to them is considerably more favorable to my survival than refusing the job."

"I see... we will have to ask you to turn over the audio record of what he asked.

"That said, do you know the name of the one who threatened you or anything about the gang's structure?"

"I do not.

"All I know is that a man named Dalton was the one who presented the deal to me.

"He never provided a last name lest it incriminates him if I told anyone."

"Makes sense.

"Guess we will have to pay him a visit later."

"So, can I go?"

"For now, the police will have to keep you under protective custody due to the facts you stated and the danger inherent to getting close to someone of that level of notoriety.

"The witness protection program, if you will.

"We just ask that you provide testimony, and we will see your safety until we have taken care of them.

"You may, however, face battery and other charges for shooting Proctavius Lee Foxx, or Proxy Foxy as he likes to be called, and attempted kidnapping."

He agreed to the terms, and somehow, we got intel on where he might be from someone on the inside, in no small part due to Bill Benson having a reputation when they served with him. A couple of people in that group want to retire in peace nowadays but cannot due to the ongoing conflict and have just enough loyalty that they must remain with the group until it disbands or they all die off.

Sure enough, we found Dalton Dredger, as his I.D. proclaimed when we rounded him up drinking at a local pub in Bakersfield. He did, however, put up a struggle, and the police helped us restrain the man, give him his Miranda rights and disarm him after we had secured the proper warrants so we could talk.

"What do you want with me? I did not do anything."

"We have reason to believe you know a man named 'Copper Furlington?'"

"Only in passing, why?"

"Because we got the word you may have been trying to abduct his kid."

"Why would we want a stupid kid?"

"It is not about the kid, but about whose kid it is and who they know."

"You may want to watch your words here.

"My allies are everywhere; even if they let you take me in, they will pick each of you off sooner or later."

"Even if you end us here, it will not stop the law from pursuing you, and it will just make it worse."

"One way or another, we will all die, and we know it.

"We put our lives on the line before you think we won't again?"

"Well, if you aren't scared to die, why not just tell us what you did?"

"Fine, yeah, I sent a guy to abduct Hunter.

"Our gang was unhappy that our friend got killed, and the guy who did it faced no repercussions.

"That meddling fox lady of yours is no help to anyone."

"She was on your side about that case."

"Bullshit!"

Suddenly a fat guy sounded like he had a bowel problem.

"Damn it stop saying that!"

"No, really, he was friends with someone who wanted a human-free world, made no denials to the fact, and was under the influence of alcohol when it happened.

"She could not prove that he did not do it in self-defense because neither of us knows what the deceased did or how they got an unregistered weapon."

"Hmm... perhaps we misjudged her.

"Still, Hunter's Father is in league with the Claws."

"And you do not think the one you sent lied to you to exact vengeance on furry kind?

"He even told us you told him what would happen if he did not do it."

"He is not wrong.

"We are a group with nothing to lose, and we aim to ensure this nation is one our kids and their grandkids can live in."

"And all this because some contractors of yours lost their man?"

"It is not about the contractor or who he was to us.

"The police are useless so long as the justice system lets criminals go free.

"We are vigilantes.

"To do that, we must be feared and respected by all."

"So, you kidnap a child with the intent to kill it?

"Is that the legacy you want to be remembered?"

"Paltry compared to the many humans who died by that two-tailed cat boy in 1994."

He spat at us.

"That was because of the organization your contractors worship."

"Bullshit! The cat boy did it, and he is lucky we never came after him, but whoever did is welcome among us."

That same fat man came towards the man waddling in his filth and us and smashed a beer bottle over our suspect, and he was out cold. A bar fight broke out, and we ran for it and called an ambulance. Then we built a case from what we could gather from him. At least he did not deny that was his plot and plan. Sure enough, the day came for the court case, but not before the man who smashed a bottle over his head got arrested for aggravated assault, battery, inciting a riot, and obstruction of justice since he was under investigation. We could not well interview him further while out cold. It was later revealed the man who hit him was named Brad Bowlcut. Ironic since he was bald when he did it. He claimed he broke a priceless record in an antique store and was hexed to lose his shit whenever someone said, "Bullshit."

Unfortunately, even if that is true, it would be impossible to prove such magic exists. For all we knew, he could have irritable bowel syndrome, especially given some of the mass quantities of bar food he was eating given the circumstances and seeming lack of intent to bother our process as much as get him to stop saying a word, the assault, battery, and obstruction of justice were treated as misdemeanors. To rise to the level of felonies, the intent must be clear they did not want justice done, and it just happened to correlate.

Moreover, inciting riot was not by any unprotected speech as much as the other charges. Thus, it was also a misdemeanor. Brad Bowlcut got a combined five years for all offenses due to how weak the case was for intent regarding obstruction of justice. The only unquestionable acts were assault and battery, which usually get six months each and fines of up to 1000 USD each. The inciting riot pretty much went the way of the assault and battery. Mr. Bowlcut did not pay them in money; instead, he paid them via added jail time.

Other patrons were given charges like being in the fray and additional riot-related charges, but none of which amounted to more than maybe a couple of months of jail time each or fines since it mainly was fist fighting and maybe spilled food and drink on one another. While insignificant to the case we aimed to investigate, they are evidence points to tack on charges against the defendant.

And that was their lengthy report pretrial for the one who conspired to kidnap and murder a kid. The fate of Carlos Diablo legally hinges significantly on the evidence we found that connects him and Dalton to the crime. While it is not quite a murder trial, I feel it would be a gross misrepresentation of the work in criminal justice if we did not show what can happen to a criminal if a murder or lesser crime is thwarted.

We now go into the courtroom at Kern County Courthouse.

Judge Sally Secular presided.

"We will now hear the case of Dalton Dredger vs. The State of California."

All parties were sworn in, and the evidence was presented. Exhibit A was the bullet Proctavius removed from his arm earlier in the chapter Exhibit B was the audio recording of the threats and instructions made to Carlos Diablo. Exhibit C photographs the blood and footprints on the crime scene. Exhibit D. The police confession and interview details, including the ensuing bar fight. Exhibit E. The forensic report and supporting documentation surrounding the evidence retrieved.

Prosecutor Gertrude Gulag began, "People of the Jury, we have a criminal before us who is not content with joining a gang of motorcyclists who disturb the peace of every decent retiree but conspired a kidnapping.

"The kidnapping of an innocent little ferret for ransom, which I remind you is in no way involved in any gangs.

"The person he hoped to avenge was not even a member of his gang but just an unrelated contractor.

"But most heinous of all, he threatened a member of the same team his gang hired to go and take a child away and whose hire shot a veteran who was protecting said child.

"These Heaven's Demons are nothing but trouble; we should make an example of him and lock him away.

"Sure, he did not kill anyone yet, but will we wait until he does?

"The evidence will show as much that this man is guilty of assault, attempted 1st-degree murder, hiring illicit services, attempted kidnapping, battery, inciting a riot, making physical threats, coercion, and that this man should ride the roads no longer."

Defense Attorney Angel Schism stated, "And I say this man was selfless and in no way liable for what transpired via his hire.

"His hire could have fled and gone to the police if these claims are valid.

"Moreover, he was interviewed while possessing and actively consuming alcohol.

"That alone should be unreliable as a confession.

"Not only that, but a rapscallion assaulted him in what culminated in a bar fight where several are serving time as we speak for misdemeanors that could have been felonies had any police killed or injured.

"It should not be Dalton here, but Carlos Diablo, whose last name means Devil in Spanish.

"The evidence will show that Dalton was nothing more than a man who sought to right a wrong in the most nonlethal way possible and could have got bad intel at worst."

Judge Sally nodded, "Very well, Proceed."

Prosecutor Gertrude continued, "Exhibit A, the bullet found inside of Proctavius, who protected the kid, and Exhibit B.

"The explicit instructions on the mission and consequences for backing down should be more than sufficient to prove coercion and intent.

"I suggest we listen to the tape to see how the two are related.

The Defense Attorney seemed a little less confident as the tape was played.

"Carlos, you have done well to gather intel on the Claws.

"I never would have suspected they had a ferret working for them behind the scenes in Torrance.

"Killing one of them in Downtown L.A. will hardly strike fear and respect in the masses.

"No, we need to go where the people have money."

"Palos Verdes?"

"No, but you are close.

"See, your project manager was supposed to build something for us, but that is not feasible on a border territory, as we discovered, so instead, we must claim new territory where there is much to steal, and no one would expect it."

"And how do you suggest we do that?"

"Simple, we abduct the child for ransom, and whether they pay us or not, they will watch in horror as the one they aimed to save is mercilessly slaughtered right in front of them.

"If you accept this mission, you could become one of us."

"You are crazy, man!

"Them having a father in the gang is hardly worth the level of terrorism you propose.

"They did not even kill my project manager.

"If we should go after anyone, it should be the Lynx that killed him.

"Then we could win support from the human masses for doing what the legal system would not."

"But you see, the justice system would be prepared for it, and the rest of the gang would be prepared for such an attack.

"However, if we go after someone completely unrelated but still affiliated, it would both accomplish revenge and be a perfect crime."

"And if I refuse and try to get help?"

"You will have no proof to demonstrate your claims.

Though the clip played on from here to go into great detail about the consequences of betrayal, I feel it is of little value to this story, and it makes me sick to try and recall it here. If you want to imagine what you consider the worst things to happen to you before death, you will have a pretty good idea of why I did not recount it here. Now that the worst part is over let us resume from the not-so-graphic part of the audio.

"Do I make myself clear?"

"Y...yes!"

"Even if you go to jail, it will not be a life sentence but maybe a few years, and while there drop our name, no one will hurt you.

"They love us in there.

"Now go to their address.

"In the middle of the night, one of our other agents got the address off an invitation the boy stupidly handed out to nearly everyone in Torrance."

The tape ended, and throughout it, the Jury looked like they would lose their lunch and cringed at the increasingly vile depictions of torture. The acts I spared you from having to read were ones that not even the most rogue of nations would have ever condoned. Not even to get information out of someone. Maybe Nazi Germany would have, but that is neither here nor there.

"So, you see, your honor, this man is a monster that needs to be locked up for the safety of all, considering what he would do to an ally if they betrayed him.

"Moreover, he did not mince words as to what he aimed to do to the child to demoralize someone only suspected of being in league with them."

Defense Attorney Angel Schism turned white as a ghost, realizing what he got himself into.

"T-that may b-be, but the one who did the real damage was not him.

"H-He, Carlos shot an agent as Exhibit A in no way disproved, and Exhibit C was the footprints of Carlos Diablo and Proctavius Foxx.

"Exhibit D, the interview on a tape recorder, and forensic evidence report Exhibit E demonstrates the blood is not on my client's hands but on anyone else."

The interview you read was played, and the Jury even heard the sound of the fight that ensued, including the man who assaulted him.

"So, you see, my client is all talk.

"Surely, if he were that dangerous, he would not have been knocked out so quickly or, barring that killed the man who knocked him out.

"He has done neither of those things, and the reports show as much."

Gertrude shook her head disapprovingly, "Drunk or not, this interview is insufficient to dispel anything Exhibit B revealed and only serves to show he has no remorse for anything he set in motion.

"Who carried out the act is irrelevant if he coerced them to do it with violent threats that a reasonable person would see as a credible threat.

"To that, I call witness Carlos Diablo via Video Call for his protection."

Carlos was sworn in, and Dalton was furious to see his face.

"Yes, the man before you threatened grievous bodily harm, and I would have instead served time under the protection of the Devil than in his path.

"Who wouldn't?"

Dalton Interjected, "Why, you sandy ass piece of animal shit!

"I ought to strangle you where you stand!

"So, help me, if I ever see you again, you are fucking dead!"

Sally banged her Gavel, "Order! The defendant will be held in contempt of court if they continue this behavior."

"Eat my ass, your dishonor!"

"That is it, I am holding him in contempt for no less than 48 hours in county jail, and we will pick this up with him properly restrained."

"Eat shit!"

"Make that 30 days."

"Get cucked!"

"120 Days"

"Blow it out your ass!"

"300 Days King Nuclear!

"Now, Bailiff, take him away so we can proceed as we were."

He struggles but stands little chance and is taken away while handcuffed after being knocked out and his leg restraints.

"I would like to apologize on behalf of my client.

"He is not in his right mind."

Judge Sally sighs, "Well, now that he is gone, perhaps we can examine the facts and our witness."

Carlos continued, "Sorry about that.

"What I was saying is apparent this guy has it in for me, and I need protection from him and his gang.

"I humbly ask the same for my other partners in the company as they could be targeted next.

"We cannot do business well under these conditions as we are already mourning the loss of our leader.

"There is not much more I can say about this that has not been mentioned.

"I mean, you saw his intent firsthand."

"That will do."

"Despite my client's behavior, he has not killed anyone since returning from the forces directly, and the prosecution cannot demonstrate different here."

"Are there any more witnesses?"

"No, your honor, I think it is clear as day anyone we would call would add nothing more than has already been said.

"You saw how he reacted right in front of you.

"Anything more would be overkill."

"Well, you are more merciful than I would be in the same situation."

Defense Attorney Angel Schism had nothing further as the Jury deliberated.

When they returned, "We find the defendant guilty of assault, attempted 1st-degree murder, hiring illicit services, attempted kidnapping, battery, inciting a riot, making physical threats, coercion, and contempt of court."

Judge Sally smiled, "Well, I am happy to say, 1st degree attempted murder alone carries a sentence of up to life in prison with the possibility of parole.

"Considering the other charges, I am inclined to rule that way.

"But should the sentence be up for parole or appeal, I will be thorough and add six months for contempt of court.

"2 years for attempted kidnapping, six months for battery, 364 days for inciting a riot.

"3 years for making physical threats in and out of court, a second life sentence for coercing a man who worked for him with graphic threats for not kidnapping a child, and 20 years for hiring a man to be a kidnapper and causing bodily harm to a search and rescue operative.

"With that, we are adjourned."

The judge banged the Gavel, and all parties left the courtroom. The defense attorney seemed somehow relieved by this. It was as if he could have been in danger or endangered many people's lives. That is, if someone of that caliber roamed free. Guess not all who defend actual criminals or prosecute against the innocent are bad.

To make a long chapter short, Carlos took a plea deal from Prosecutor Gertrude Gulag after much negotiation. He pleaded guilty to the misdemeanor Simple Battery for shooting Proctavius Foxx in exchange for three years probation instead of imprisonment. The deal was offered to him because he cooperated in the case against Dalton Dredger. With that, we close this chapter most satisfyingly. I hope you are as excited to see what the next chapter holds.

CHAPTER 9

HUNTING FOR THE TRUTH

Outgunned & Outfoxed

After that dramatic court case surrounding a crime with no dead bodies, it was back to business as usual. After some convincing, Bill managed to get the Furlington family to let their son stay with Proctavius for his protection. I had not thought much about how oddly specific it was that Don Giovanni mentioned there might be a conspiracy to mix people of his friends' backgrounds in murder investigations. This leads us to this chapter's case.

Remember Henry Skins? He had been murdered in his home. I had to figure out who did it alongside my usual team. The neighbors across the fence would have been the obvious suspect. Suicide from the pressure of all he killed when he was a soldier? No, it had to be something more.

"Lailah thank Bast you are here."

"What is it, Mr. Sleuth?"

"Preliminary findings show the cause of death to be an arrow."

"What, but who?"

"Well, there is a national park near where the man lived where archery is a popular sport.

“Perhaps we could find some answers there.”

So, after sending the evidence found at the man’s house, the arrowhead some of the various trophies of feral animals he slew, to name a few items, we made our way to Yosemite National Park. A couple of pretty young-looking foxes practiced different ranged arts: archery and knife throwing. Tough as the arts they practiced, it was somehow cute to see them fostering interests like that so soon as if a child thinking they are all grown up but not knowing what it means to be an adult. I turned to one that finished a round of arrows.

"Hey there, I am Lailah."

“Kit Kit, and the one throwing knives is Kit Kat.”

“Cute, but uh, question, what got you both into such hobbies?”

“This world will kill you if you do not learn skills to defend yourself, or do you not watch the news?”

“I investigate those kinds of cases.”

“Amusing... lot of good it does em when they are the corpse.”

“Who hurt you?”

“Dunno? See anyone with a menagerie of skins anywhere?”

“Is that supposed to be funny?”

“No, why?”

“I happen to be on a case investigating who put an arrow through his head! And yes, he had his share of skins.”

“Ironic, but he probably deserved it.

"Can’t just shoot living things dead and not expect to die.”

“While I see your point, you eat meat too by species.”

“Yeah, but I am not the one killing it.

"No use wasting what will not be revived no matter what we do.”

“Kit Kit, can you quit being a tail hole for one second?

"She was admiring us for being so grown up.”

“No, Kit Kat, she aims to lock us up for the death of someone we had no involvement in.”

“Both of you calm down.

"I do not intend to put either of you away, and I want to ask if you know anyone who has been acting out of sorts that might have had the propensity to do what you think I want to pin on you."

Kit Kit nodded, "Dunno if it helps, but I saw a human watching us a little too closely.

"I cannot say whether he did, but he could likely have mimicked and learned from us."

"Any features stand out about him?"

"He was a man in his 60s from the looks of it.

"I followed him once and saw him making swords with a forge like in old times."

"So, he could have been studying you for weapons crafting or plotting something."

"Perhaps it was all we saw, though I am doubtful it would be them.

"It is too obvious."

"Sadly, you are correct."

Just when all hope seemed lost, I tripped over a clue. It was a sign felled by strong winds.

"Axel Flask's Medieval Might." Hmm, a weapon shop, perhaps? A man excused himself and pointed to the sign I was holding. He matched the description the kits gave.

"Oh, this is your sign?"

"Mhm... names Axel... Axel Flask.

"I sell medieval-style weapons, though be careful these things can cut you if you try anything stupid.

"You must be the age of majority for your species or have your parent purchase them for you."

I handed him his sign, unsure how evidentiary value would be assessed on a simple signboard. Watching him lay out his wares and set up shop, I noticed he had crossbows and arrows among the swords and shields. I phoned Cat Sleuth and the rest of the team, who showed up within a couple hours or so as they had been hanging around Yosemite Village while I made my way in for other clues, or so they said.

"Leonard, I am glad you are here, and you too, Patrick."

"Well, now that the gangs are all here for the second time today, what have you discovered?"

"It seems that this here weaponsmith in front of us might know something about how his weapons work, and I wanted some experts in inquisition to help piece this together.

"You 3 are the best in the business when it comes to that, while I find clues in physical things."

PI Patrick Patterson was the first to approach the merchant.

"Such shiny wares you have here.

"Might I get a good look at them?"

"Sure, I got many types to go over, but our traditional oak crossbow is one of our best sellers.

"Sturdy and long-lasting for hours of target practice.

"Just do not use it on the living."

Overhearing this, I pieced together what I saw on the scene an arrow that looked just like the kind sold here, but who would have bought it and then done that and would think he could get away with it?

Patrick Patterson went in next. "Mighty fine blades indeed, and that crossbow looks like it was made in ye olden times."

Axel looked my way and stared, suspicious of my friends' seemingly workshopped dialog.

"Alright, I think I know what is going on here.

"Someone disobeyed my terms and conditions on using one of these crossbows."

Knowing the jig was up, I stepped forward, "That is correct, I am loathed to trouble you, and I like your weapons.

"However, someone got killed via one of those archery sets, and we were prepared to offer you payment on behalf of our investigative firm.

"We just need information that helps us bring justice to the slain."

"Very well, though I find it a little insulting you think it would take money to get me to spill what I know.

"Though I understand you know the time value of money."

"Yeah, we found this guy we had interrogated in a previous case.

"We thought he accidentally killed someone while drunk with friends.

"He was found recently with an arrow through his head.

"So, we looked for any place that might sell the model of the used archery set.

"The furnish on yours was 100% the match in every way.

"The color, the curvature.

"We do not believe you had anything to do with it.

"However, if we had a name of anyone you sold things to for crime record lookups and past juvenile history, it would be swell."

"There was one man.

"He brought his kid out here to get an archery set to practice the sport like that fox boy.

"No, I did not sell it directly to the kid.

"His parent signed the release and purchased it for him.

"Same with the one, I suspect.

"Well, as much as his dad seemed to love archery, his son seemed bored by the prospect.

"Wondering the use of such a thing when hunting is illegal here.

"There was nothing to suggest either came from the environment where one would have unresolved anger.

"Just your average run-of-the-mill father trying to push a sport the son has no interest.

"The father's name was Herbert Harbinger XIII, and the Son Herbert Harbinger XIV."

"Sounds ominous."

"Maybe, but the rich folk have weird ideas for naming sometimes."

"Well, thanks for the intel.

"Here's a small sum for your time."

I handed him the money as promised and noticed myself tempted by some of his merchandise. What can I say? Though hardened by my line of work, I admire someone with strong attention to detail and authenticity when making items.

"Oh! While I am here, I think I will take an archery set.

"You have an archer tunic too?

"Okay, one of those, too, please."

Leonard shook his head disappointedly, "Lailah, you gave into your gatherer impulse.

"You need to watch it if you want to retire."

"Please, I wear the same outfit almost every day and have a nearly empty closet at home, given the nature of our work.

"We never know when we must pack up and run."

With that, we made our way to the Mansion atop the hill. The man seemed delighted to have company, the son not so much.

"Welcome, guests.

"Might I offer thee a spot of tea?"

"Thanks for the offer, but we are here to see your son."

"Oh, friends of his, eh?"

I could not tell if he was being clever with us or not all there.

"Well, you know what, maybe it is better if we discuss this over tea.

"It has been a long day."

He rang his bell, and a Butler Cat came out.

"You called Master?"

"Yes, Whiskens, might you pour our humble guests a spot of tea?"

"Bedouin Chai, sir?"

"Oh yes, that would be fabulous!"

"One moment, sir."

The cat person returns to the kitchen and brings out tea and milk, his kid sitting pouting.

"Hey there, little one, you, okay?"

No response.

"Oh, never mind, my son.

"He can be a bit of a sourpuss, heh."

"Heh yeah, goes with the territory, I suppose."

As the tea is served, I, with my best social grace, sip it like a proper lady. I do not know what made me feel sicker, the carefree attitude of Mr. Harbinger XIII, or the appropriate lady act I felt compelled to do in search of information.

Leonard interjected, "I think what Lailah is getting at is children can have their moods.

"Sometimes it stems from a lack of attention from parents or being placed into activities they have no interest in?"

"Oh, I see... well, I loved the art of firing arrows at inanimate objects to try and hit the center target.

"I used to be among the best at it and won my share of awards.

"I had hoped my little one would have taken to it, but it seems not."

"That happens all too often.

"By the way, if I may, I want to talk to your son privately.

"I am a psychologist, and I can help you find out how to connect with him a little more."

"Splendid! I would love nothing more than to put a smile on my little one's face."

Leonard escorted him to the next room and recorded the conversation.

"Hello, Herbert XIV. I understand your dad tried to push a sport on you that you did not like."

"Yeah..."

"Well, do you have any sports you like?"

"Not really... kids make fun of me no matter what sport I try.

"I will never be legendary at anything."

"You do not have to be.

"You just have to be you and not give a damn about anything others think."

"Everyone tells me that, but they would quickly change their tune if they knew what makes me who I am."

"Oh, are you implying deep down you are some sort of demon from hell or something?"

"No, but I am pretty sure I would not be making Santa's nice list if he had any window into my soul, so to speak."

"Why do you say that?"

"Inside me is pure unadulterated hate.

"I hate these air-headed, out-of-touch people that live around here.

"But more than them, I hate people who keep carcasses of animals on their wall like it makes them more manly."

"That is strangely specific.

"Did you know anyone like that?"

"Yeah, my old man had him over for tea the other day.

"I do not know if you noticed, but he seems completely without any street smarts, or he would have known what you all are here for."

"And what is it we are here for?"

"You all think I killed him...that I killed Mr. Skins."

"We do not think that, but this home is where the trail of evidence has led."

"I admit, I shot a few arrows at his 'precious' trophies a few times, but I would never aim to end another life."

"So, you admit to Vandalism, but do you know how he could have got one of your arrows into his head?"

"It was an accident, okay?

"I was aiming to spook the guy as a prank by firing one at a target he had in his backyard.

"The idiot put his lawn chair too close to it.

"While aiming for the target, I expected him not to wake until after I hit it.

"His chair was off the right side, so I aimed as far left as possible.

"The wind picked up, and he got up to go inside on my left.

"That was when I fired my shot, and well, I am pretty sure you saw the state he was in."

"So, you accidentally killed him via headshot due to a wrong prank?"

"Yes...while I think he deserved to die for his crimes against nature, I never meant to be the one to do it."

"How old are you, son?"

He held up six digits, "This many."

"Well, if it is any relief, I can tell you.

"For being honest and too young to have the mental faculties for intending to murder in the eyes of the law, you likely will not serve jail time.

"If anything, you might be put in a children's mental hospital depending on how dangerous they think you are or put in foster care if your parent is deemed negligent.

"But more than likely, you will just be forbidden from leaving home for some years at worst to protect the general public.

"With how well-to-do your dad is, you might even get off without much repercussion, especially if you win over the jury's sympathy.

"So, if it were me, I would lose the sour attitude when the case happens.

"Consider it free advice from someone who has seen how these things play out.

"Regardless, you are a much better person for coming clean about this.

"Also, do not talk to the police when they come except to ask for a Lawyer present for questioning."

According to Leonard, he nodded understanding and was in tears, realizing the gravity of what he had done.

That was the end of the recording. I may not have liked Herbert XIV's attitude before, but now I understand why he was so defensive. When the evidence sent to the lab came back, including photos, it seemed his archery set was behind the crime. Also, considering where the body lay compared to his confession and the target he had set up for ranged weapon training, it would seem plausible that the kid was aiming for the target, not him. Henry Skins also occasionally liked to hunt with a bow and arrow and set targets in his backyard. Maybe it was after he nearly got in trouble for shooting cans a few chapters ago. Regardless things proceeded as usual, and he indeed took the advice. This leads us to the scene in court.

Samantha Stockade was the prosecution attorney, Kevin Key was the defense attorney, and judge was Simon South Sea.

"Alright, we will hear the case of Herbert XIV vs. the State of California. All parties have been sworn in.

"Let us begin."

Samantha Stockade nodded, "Thank you, your honor.

"This seemingly innocent boy has committed a crime most foul.

"He killed a legendary war hero who partially defeated the Aryan Brotherhood of Germany or the original Nazi party.

"And it was this spoiled brat of a child I have half a mind to choke to death right here that did the deed, or so the evidence will show."

Kevin key then made his case, "And I say the evidence will show the boy lacked the mental wherewithal to intentionally kill a man in cold blood.

"Thus, the death was an accident while perpetrating a juvenile misdemeanor of trespass and vandalism at worst."

"Very well, then proceed."

"Exhibit A the confession the boy did the deed and his intent.

"Exhibit B is the archery set and bloodied arrow that matches it.

"And Exhibit C The forensic report and detective findings of the scene that line up perfectly with the crime.

"The evidence alone makes this an open and shut case."

"Except for one thing, we are not contesting that the deed was done by him, but was it intentional and thus manslaughter or Murder, or was it, at best, an unforeseen accident?

"To that end, I call Forensic Psychologist Leonard Rudder-Butt."

A few snickers came from the defendant.

"That's Rudder-Beaut!

"How is it you are in the remembering of the Leonard and the Rudder part but not the Beautiful part?"

"Sorry, Rudder-Beaut!

"Anyways, you are an expert Psychologist.

"Skilled at knowing how young minds work, and is it safe to say you have worked on your share of cases?"

"Yes, to everything you just said."

"Then tell me.

"Is the brain of a 6-year-old child capable of having the foresight to anticipate possibly causing grievous bodily harm?

"To the extent all life leaves one, should a prank of theirs backfire as it did?"

"No, their sense of cause and effect has been scientifically proven both psychologically and physiologically not to be fully developed in humans at the tender age of 6."

"So, you are suggesting they have enough to know that if they do not feed their pets, they die, but it is insufficient to predict someone will wake up and get killed by an arrow?

"I remind the court, no one has thus far disputed the order of events but whether this is something a reasonable child would grasp."

"That is correct.

"This archery accident was nothing more than a child's prank gone wrong from what I made of his statements on Exhibit A.

"While not my place to officially decide, I do not believe he deserves to spend time in Juvenile Hall.

"But house arrest with community service would be appropriate to ensure no one else is hurt and confiscation of his weapon.

He should have his weapon back once he is old enough to know how not to kill someone with it as an adult would accidentally."

Kevin Key nodded, "Sounds very reasonable to me.

"Now, what say the Prosecution to this claim?"

"Six years old or six hundred years old makes little difference.

"We still have a war hero laid in his grave by a reckless child, and we should not let them get off lightly because then they will kill again."

Simon Southsea interjected, "Unfortunately, even if data on a child's preponderance for cause and effect is limited.

"The current system sees them as being akin to infants.

"So, unless I see intent to harm beyond a shadow of a doubt, it is unlikely we will be able to do much.

"We could have CPS remove the child from home and delay their right to possess arms."

"You have got to be kidding me!

"This kid knows what he did as per the tape, and you are just going to let it go?"

"I do not make the rules.

"I just enforce them.

"Now that we know none of the evidence is contested and have heard arguments from both of you who realize the limitations involved in this case, I say we move to close Statements."

Samantha Stockade looking nearly defeated, "What the Jury must realize is age, or not a crime was committed here.

"No one is contesting that much.

"The question is, what do we do about it?

"At the very least, we should charge him on Trespass and Vandalism, which he admitted to on tape."

Keven Key said, "And I say he does not deserve to have the rest of his life ruined by accident.

"Fine, let him do some good for the community or be limited where he can go, but putting him in Juvenile Hall will only make him worse.

"He will probably need intensive therapy to get over the guilt of what he has done."

"Has the jury reached a verdict?"

"On the counts of Murder and Manslaughter, he is not guilty.

"Due to his age, we deem him not guilty of felony trespass and vandalism but do find him guilty of misdemeanor trespass and destruction of property."

"Very well then, as suggested by the suitable Psychologist, I will sentence them to trauma therapy for PTSD and anything else they diagnose him.

"I further order he be forced to remain at home when not performing supervised community service for two years or at appointments or other essential supervised things.

"He will be educated privately following it.

"No ranged or melee weapon training is permitted either.

"Lastly, his family will pay a fine equal to the funeral costs of any remaining family to bury and mourn him. Since they can afford it, a restitution equal to a full-ride scholarship to an accredited University in the State to each of Henry Skin's grandchildren is to be paid when they are old enough to enter college.

"That is all."

With the bang of the gavel, we are adjourned.

Though less imprisonment happened, the judge was hard on them for the funeral and college. At least this gives them time to prepare their finances for it, though. I did not want him to suffer jail time either, but hopefully, Herbert XIII and Herbert XIV learned a valuable lesson from this and would not be involved in crime again. At least time will tell, but that is all for this chapter.

CHAPTER 10

STRAINS OF INSANITY

Stranger things are happening.

Before we begin this chapter's case, let me preface this and say things have been rather weird lately, as you may have noticed, but it has mostly been tame up to now. Today was the day I turned on my TV to notice the more racially charged rhetoric now allowed to air that had not been seen since the 1960s.

On FTV, they aired a rather disturbing joke PSA. "This is a PSA from your local Doctor, Rob Tarker.

"The human population far exceeds any animal on the planet Earth.

"If you are a furry who owns a human, help us control the human population and have your human spayed or neutered today!

"For more information, call: 1-800-This-Is-A-Joke Thank you"

And then the News came on.

"Good morning, Generic News Viewers!

"It is Saturday Morning, but crime never takes a day off, so neither does this news station.

"Our first story is a bill passed by Congress to separate the Human Postal Services from the Furry Postal Services.

"The two services now operate as HPS for Human Parcel Service, and for Furries, it is USPSPSPSPSPSPS, and its icon is a cat.

"Hahahaha, just kidding, this has been our 'Silly Saturdays' segment.

"The post office is still the post office.

"In more pressing News, a corporate Supply Store data breach was believed to be behind the death of a couple of families, one of which is in Miami, Florida, and the other in Dallas, Texas.

"The suspect is still at large but left a note reading, 'Steal my Credit Line, Lose your Life Line.'

"Payfiend declined to comment, but complaints about the credit and payment processing solution state that they would have scammers get away with fraudulent charges and not step in when needed.

"Especially true when purchases are made at known shops. These problems persist while Payfiend collects nearly 3% or more of the value of each transaction.

"It makes you wonder how they are still in business, but I suppose what they say is true.

"'A sucker is born every minute.'

"And this has been Generic News. We will be right back after a commercial."

Yeesh, time to watch something more wholesome for a change.

My job bums me out enough as it is without negative News.

I changed the channel to Kids Channel 3. On it, they had kids too young for school hours with the Same Old Avenue show. I blacked out, listening to a Mortician counting flowers in his cemetery, laughing at random intervals as he did. It hardly felt like I had blacked out, and it felt like I was still conscious.

The next thing I knew, I saw the show was still on, but the cast had been lying lifeless on the ground as a figure I swear I saw in chapter two hopped around like a puppet.

He said, "This program has been brought to you by the letter F for Forsaken and number 666."

He laughed as the TV did a red scene transition bringing us to a room where skeletal versions of the puppets sang along with him.

"'F' is for Forsaken that took all our lives.

"'F' is for Forsaken that took all our lives.

"'F' is for Forsaken, who took all our lives.

"Oh Forsaken, Forsaken, Forsaken starts with F!"

I saw a pair of cat paws come out of the TV and jolt awake to see I had somehow flipped the channel to the horror one where they had Sofer reading a scary short story about a cat boy who found a book of undead and destroyed two cities.

Still waking up, I barely processed the entirety of it, but I swear I heard them say, "Mom's not here, kids!

"Yes, scream for me. Your pain, your agony sustains me!

"You may think your authorities stand up for what is right, but you are mistaken."

Somehow it all sounded too familiar though I swear it never happened. Then I thought about Adam; he had not sent me a letter before I almost lost my vehicle in a riot, and I began to worry just a little. I hoped he was okay wherever he might have been. Just then, my day off was interrupted by a phone call.

"Lailah, we have a new case for you on Catalina Island.

"Don't Enjoy yourself too much.

"We have also paid to let you stay in the Loner Forest Campsite."

"Couldn't afford me a hotel this time?"

"Don't push it.

"Our unit's budget has been cut due to current racial tensions.

"If anything happens to your car, it is up to you to find a way to fix it, so leave it locked securely away at home where it is now."

"Yeah, I am aware it is being monitored. Let's hope no one within the organization uses that against us."

"You read too many mystery novels, haven't you?"

"I am joking, sir!

"Seriously, that would be way too predictable."

"Sometimes the best criminals are the ones you dismiss from the outset for being too obvious.

"Most of them are not that good at covering their tracks.

"Your cases are a mixed bag from what we have seen."

"Right..."

"Now get to it, Rookie."

Hmph, "Rookie."

Fine, I only worked on 9 cases worth writing about, but many more people got put away who deserved it with my help forensic work that stood less of a chance of getting away with it.

I could not pay my bills well if all my cases were as high profile and dramatic as the ones in this novel.

Though I digress.

I made my way to the Catalina 1 Hour boat. On it, I showed my ticket, and within an hour, I was on the Avalon side of Catalina Island. When the description said the case occurred in a Casino, I thought it would be some gambling house and an entertainment venue that shows movies on Wednesdays. It gets its name because, in Italian, Casino means "gathering place." I went to the campsite I was checked into, and they got my team and me the tent cabins, so we slept on hammock beds for up to 10 people.

"Ah, pretty nice to escape the city for a while, Lailah?"

"Yeah, Leonard, a little too peaceful here. It worries me a little."

"Oh, come now, Lailah, it is your paranoia again."

"Tell me, Cat, have you had to have anyone you befriend outside of work get abducted for their protection?

"Did you end up in an escape game show with your team on vacation?

"Okay, you did because we were in that one together.

"Did you have your emergency vehicle almost stolen while a riot broke over a case you worked on?"

"No to all, except the one we were in together by your admission.

"Nevertheless, I do not try to make friends with people on the outside.

"It makes solving cases too complicated and emotional.

"Moreover, I do not have to report to courts in any of these cases, so you should leave the vehicle locked up except in an emergency that needs it.

"They have public transit in every part of the State practically."

"True, I suppose bringing the UP convertible vehicle is my problem when I could afford a regular car like everyone else has with my salary.

"Still, I loathe spending 8 hours haggling with sleazy car salesmen."

Patrick, ever the jokester, quoted some fake TV Ad, "Welcome to Honest Mack Car Purgatory.

"If you think you are in for a great deal on a new or used car this summer, you can blow it out your tail hole!

"That's right, blow it out your tail hole!

"We think you are a dumb schmuck who will stop at nothing to acquire a vehicle with License Plate 'Sucks 2B U!'

"And here at Honest Macks Car Purgatory, we are home of challenge spitting!

"If you can spit 10 feet in the air and swallow it without getting wet on your face, we will give you no down payment!

"So, what are you waiting for, you lousy piece of elephant dung?

"Get down here now!"

"If only they were that honest, I would be more inclined to pay the sticker price."

Lovely as the cabin tent was, daylight was burning, so we put on our work boots and got to the scene.

The local island police guarded the crime scene until we showed our clearance, and then we began our investigation.

I was the first to speak, "Hmm, the body here appears well-preserved.

"But it seems like the cause of death was not any specific weapon, but what could have done it?"

PI Patrick scratched his chin, "Judging from his personal effects, it seems he went to a few bars from the receipts in his wallet, but we will need to send the body in for autopsy since it does not appear anything around him was likely to have done him in.

"His name is Theodore Journeyman, age 35, and according to our records has no known criminal activity but one dependent.

Species is Raccoon, but who would want this guy dead and why?"

Cat said, "No idea, but if we can go to a few places they went, maybe we can sleuth some clues."

Leonard nodded, "Right."

Leonard and Patrick split up to ask different places what had been going on and came back with some interesting intel. From the notes both had written, Theodore had just finished a Business deal on the island with their owners to have his company work on the electrical grid on the island to update it so they could better keep up with the 21st-century power needs. The business location is out of San Pedro, California, known as "Let There Be Light." It should come as little surprise given the shipyard that could take him to Catalina, not to mention the refineries and industrial complexes in the surrounding area. The body was sent back to the lab for an autopsy. Tomorrow we will search for clues about his company property.

Until then, we hailed a vehicle service that specifically took tourists to a popular restaurant and bar on the island Wild Cow Quarter. There we had what else but burgers, and even I let my hair down with their specialty cocktail, Wild Cow Milk. It was delicious and reminded me a little of a White Russian or a milkshake with alcohol.

After my morning's nightmare, I figured a little nerve relaxant might help me sleep better despite our minimalist accommodations. I will have to remember this place if I ever get to go on vacation again.

Unfortunately, me being an infrequent drinker and my comrades as well, we had some, I will say, "interesting" discussions.

"S-so I said to him, no man, if I were in love with another, I would be known as the black widow."

"Why is that?"

"Cause the way things are going, they gonna disappear sooner or later and be presumed dead, ha!"

"That is what my doctor said about my-"

A group "Woah" sound interrupted and censored that unclean thought. Yeah, safe to say the rest of the conversations were not much more PG than that. We finished our food and drink and spent the night telling campfire stories until we passed out on our cots. The following day we took our boat back to the mainland with nothing further to investigate.

The team quickly made a beeline for the company known as "Let There Be Light."

At the company, a nearly identical man to the one we found dead on the island but significantly younger was leading things in the facility's main building.

"Alright, men, Theodore has not returned yet from Catalina Island and has not responded to my pager or any attempts to reach out.

"I must go there to ensure all is well and the contract went through."

Then we came in, and I explained what we had found, including the contract signed by the company.

"I figured, which is why it is a good thing the contract stipulated in the event of the signer's death, all living members will go ahead with the project as planned.

"He also let us in on the plan to upgrade the island so we can proceed from there."

"You seem calm about this.

"You did just lose your father, didn't you?"

"He taught me always to put work first and shove it down until the job is done."

"Ah, a stoic."

"Call it what you will, but mourning a loss won't pay our salaries or pay for the burial, for that matter."

PI Patrick interjected, "Did your dad have any enemies?

"Maybe some rivals who would gain from him being taken out of the picture?"

"Not to my knowledge.

"We are all contractors who work for our own.

"In a way, we are all owners of this company by way of our work.

"We all have health benefits as if employees of a bigger firm but otherwise, the company's culture is pretty open to doing whatever side projects one wants between current contracts."

"I see... has Theodore been taking any kind of medications?"

"He tried some antidepressants, but they seemed pretty ineffective.

"He is also known for excessive consumption of alcohol, so it would not surprise me if he ticked someone off.

"Nor would it if the one he ticked off sprinkled something extra in one of his drinks."

"That is oddly specific..."

"It is speculation, and I am no detective, but if the cause of death is not something to do with a weapon, perhaps a toxicology check is in order?"

Suddenly my pager buzzed, indicating the sample was ready for examination.

"Well, I will leave you all here to talk things over. I need to go back to the lab and draft a report of the findings."

Quickly, I borrowed the PI's regular car and returned to the lab. When I got back, I examined the remains and performed my tests. Sure enough, as the son suggested, there had been trace amounts of a toxic substance. Thallium Poisoning. For those unfamiliar with chemistry or too lazy to google it, Thallium in lethal doses can be administered to a victim, and it could take up to 5 days to kill someone. It is odorless and flavorless; no one would suspect anything is amiss until it is too late. In safer doses, it can remedy Syphilis. This makes tracing the killer hard in these types of cases. They could well have fled the country by now unless they got cocky.

Less fatal symptoms occur within 6 hours, such as severe abdominal pain, cramping, diarrhea, and vomiting. Indeed, he would have tried to go to the ER with those symptoms alone, and it would have been discovered. Perhaps if he had it with alcohol, he could have dismissed it as regular food poisoning or alcohol intoxication. So strange...

I got a call from the PI, "Lailah, we have a clue who the killer might have been."

"Who?"

"Remember how a furry killed a person, a Paws member killed someone?"

"Yeah."

"Well, we have reason to believe someone was furious about that, and this was a retaliation on a seemingly random furry."

"Though we have already solved a case like that, it is still a hasty conclusion.

"What makes you say that?"

"Well, as you remember, Lionus Lynx was an ally of the Claws.

"We have gathered that the victim recently did building projects on their compound.

"The Heaven's Demons did not take kindly to that faction and were even less happy to see Mr. Lynx went free despite killing a human who was a friend of theirs and performed a similar role with his firm."

"After their botched kidnapping and murder plot of a suspected member of the Claws' son, it would seem another redoubled their efforts to take a life for a life."

"So, it sounds like a mix of gang and company warfare."

"That is about the size of it."

"Great, just when I thought things couldn't be more complicated."

"I feel you, but we are getting close to the truth."

"And then what?

"More retaliation and more cases to solve?"

"Lailah, I know this is frustrating, but we need to do this.

"It may lead to what you figured, but it may not.

"The key is people are counting on us to see we do all we can to bring all criminals to justice no matter who they serve and the outcome."

"You are right.

"Besides, it is what we are paid to do.

"I just hate how no matter what we do, this is very much an exercise of politics."

"It has always been that way.

"It is more the center of debate now than it was for a time."

Without further exchange, I returned the PI's car to him, and he gave me his notes to combine with his findings. As a quick recap, as it has been a couple of chapters since the last case involving them, Heaven's Demons see themselves as Super Heroes or Vigilantes rather than a gang. The Paws behave similarly but give justice a chance, and the Claws are the furry version of Heaven's Demons without the military background but do not seem to let it hold them back.

If that were not headache enough, many humans love Heaven's Demons, and if we learned nothing from last time, investigating them will cause a stir. While there are traitors among them, the vow to keep secrets at all costs means we would need to get them alone or drunk to have any hope of extracting information from them, as force is unlikely to phase them.

However, if we had Bill Benson work his magic again, perhaps we could obtain forensic clues or get some leads.

Sure enough, Bill Benson was on it before I could ask him. While he set off for it, I went home for the day, as did the rest of my team. The next day Mr. Benson, like a miracle worker, had our next lead.

"Lailah, it seems like our suspect has been found."

"Oh?"

"The Heavens Demons have had their eyes on a former member, a traitor.

"His name is 'Thaddius Yu.'"

"What?

"I thought that was just a conspiracy.

"A tall tale told to instill fear in him."

"I thought so too.

"I once reported to him for weapons in the war.

"I knew he lacked empathy for others, but I did not think he was that evil.

"Go find him and take this with you.

"He may be armed and dangerous."

I was given a UP-issued defense gun, Model 1. Model one uses ammunition right for Earth's level of development—no lasers or obvious sci-fi stuff. If anything, it is more comparable with a standard earth handgun. However, it has specific ammo meant to penetrate bullet-proof armor and deactivate tanks and other machinery via electronic signals while leaving them intact for repossession and reactivation."

"I usually do not give such items to people working for me, but your United Planets insisted I protect you and other furry personnel.

"Otherwise, the alliance is off.

"Which means we will never be trusted with cool tech like hover cars, to name one.

"I rather like flying cars, personally.

Your teammates also have a gun like yours, now go find the truth."

I nodded and went forward with the mission. In retrospect, I should have foreseen that being sent on a mission dangerous enough to warrant any gun might be a trap.

I went to the address of Thaddius Yu that the boss gave on Alcatraz Island. It seems the war and his tech position afforded him the buying power to buy the former prison island, and it serves as a tourist attraction which likely brings in even more money to cover the cost. Some friendly human tour guides approached me upon entering the island.

"Welcome to Alcatraz Island!

"Have you come for a tour?

"It is only $200 admission per person."

We showed our badges, they seemed to understand, and Thaddius came out unarmed to talk to us.

"Oh, hello, Lailah.

"I heard much about you, PI Patrick, Leonard, Cat Sleuth.

"You all showed up here with weapons.

"This must be serious."

"Yeah, we were told you were ruthless regarding war machines."

"Oh, not at all.

"They just admired my skill in weapons creation, as all should.

"We have a hall of war machines and weapons decommissioned.

"You do get your bang for your buck here."

"What do you know about the Heaven's Demons?"

He made a "you should not have said that" face and gestured to a private room. We followed him suspiciously.

"We must never speak their name publicly; the mere utterance of it could alert them to us.

"Anyone around you could be someone who would stop at nothing to join their gang, but they are selective and live by a code of secrecy.

"I made the mistake of trying to join decades ago, thinking they were just a motorcycle club, and I loved their leather jackets.

"Back then, loyalty and swearing to secrecy was much more followed.

"Given that I had already shown my fearlessness in building and repairing weapons while fired upon as was expected, they quickly let me into their ranks.

"I was among the first to know that they use what they learned in war to earn street credit and whatever they want.

"However, no one could foresee the rats that would soon breed mistrust among the ranks and enter the witness protection program.

"One notable one was the one you might know by his alias Assn the Assassin."

Lailah looking appalled, "So you are suggesting the case where nearly all evidence showed he had killed someone it was framed as self-defense and nevermind the fact he was stalking a property?"

"Exactly that.

"The fact he even went on trial at all was only to drive away suspicion he had any legal immunity in the witness protection program."

"Then what is the use of the legal system?"

"Do not worry unless he has jobs from the government to do.

"We house him here.

"So, he faces legal repercussions for his deeds while under it.

"We use a military prison system to isolate him from other prisoners.

"In exchange for him doing the Government's dirty work, we protect him from the gangs by hiding his residency here."

He showed us the old prison cells behind the authorized-personnel-only area. The missing suspect from Chapter 2 was in the cell next to his with his last name on it.

"Hello, Lailah"

"How do you know my name, Mc Coy?"

"It is on the prison TV those court cases are televised for the public, and we watch you testify."

"And you, you killed Mr. Hatfield, didn't you?"

"Technically not.

"I just gave some orphans the guns and told them where to hang out; then I let their true nature take hold.

"It was a risk, but I knew that whoever they hit would stick it to the man for outsourcing my department to a bunch of sand people to save money and avoid paying pensions to people like me.

"I had one year of work to earn it, damn it all!"

"So, how did you wind up here?"

"Thaddius Yu understood my anger at him and agreed to keep me here for the time I would have served on the outside.

"He pulled some strings to give me a new identity to avoid serving time with many brutes who would kill me on day 1.

"Suppose I survived jail, and it would be near impossible with a criminal record to get hired anywhere else.

"Not helped is I am much older, and most places want people in their 20s or 30s on their team when hiring.

"Now I get nothing because he made a bullshit reason to fire my whole team.

"Because we were fired and not laid off or allowed to retire, none of us even get a fraction of what we would have had if we had remained just one more year.

"Disgusting!

"And after all, my team and I did for the man."

"I am so sorry he did that to you."

"Unfortunately, the law cares nothing for aggravating circumstances regarding acquittal.

"Never mind that I may only have 20-30 more years of life if I am lucky, given the average human life expectancy.

"Fortunately, Thaddius has a heart and agreed to let me serve my time and have top-of-the-line elder care and all needs met for food, money, and much more the old stiff would not let me have.

"He is even sponsoring my children's education and recommending them for scholarships, so their life will be nice once mine ends."

Thaddius turned to me, "You could have all that and better if you join us and keep the information we just gave you a secret.

"We may not be affiliated with Heavens Demons anymore, but we can make your life enviable.

"Or you could try to leave and hope we did not plan for you to be a straight shooter.

"Take your time and discuss it, but remember we are watching you once you leave here."

I said, "This might be why our boss gave us these."

Leonard said, "But if we pull them out, this guy could be ready for it, and our fates are sealed."

Cat said, "I never was good at deception, but maybe..."

P.I. Patrick stepped forth and spoke for us, "Okay, we will keep your secret.

"I see a beautiful tourist attraction here and nothing more."

I interjected, "I guess you got us in a corner.

"We know your secret, but if we tried to tell, we would die.

"Even if we tried to fight back and survived, we would surely be on trial for anyone who died.

"And how would we prove our innocence and this top-secret place?

"Well, check, mate, I guess."

"I knew you would see things my way."

My fox ears twitched, hearing something from a distance.

"You hear something, Lailah?"

Suddenly Thaddius clutched his chest and fell. We looked at each other and took cover behind whatever looked sturdy, expecting whatever shot at him to shoot again. Before long, the police entered our room.

"Freeze!"

We put up our paws and remained silent, as was our right. We knew how this looked. We had two people kidnapped in cells, and we were out and able to go where we wanted was what any reasonable person who just came in would think, knowing nothing of what we saw and heard. We knew resisting arrest would just make things worse. Besides, we could get our boss to tell them we did not do this and had a valid reason to be here.

The following scene takes place in the Inquisition room.

"So, you maintain that you did not shoot the man?

"You were sent to interview this guy and investigate his former prison island?

"There you found those two caged up, and they were but provided for at his expense?

"Then suddenly he was felled by a projectile none of you shot and heard only due to your animal sense of hearing?"

We all nodded.

"You expect us to believe that?"

Each of us shrugged.

Our boss came in, "I am disappointed in all of you.

"I thought none of you would have done something like this."

He checked our arms which were confiscated.

"None of you pulled the trigger?"

The police turned to Bill Benson.

"You gave them the weapons and sent them there?"

"I told them to investigate Thaddius and to keep those weapons on them due to the heightened risk of life and limb that comes with the kinds of cases they work on.

"I never told them to use them or not.

"It is their sole discretion to use as needed if threatened, but none of them fired a single shot, although the man is... very much dead.

"Issue is now that they have become a suspect in this case and will have a trial to prove what we know before a court, I have no choice but to take them off this case until they can be found not guilty.

"If they are found guilty, I have no choice except to terminate their employment."

Sorry folks, it looks like this case just turned into a Two-Parter. The next chapter will begin with our court hearing, and maybe we will find out who shot Thaddius. But hey, what a twist, am I right?

CHAPTER 11

A TALE OF TWO TRIALS

Or Four, Maybe More

Welcome back. In the last chapter, we were interrogated about our involvement, and our Boss showed up to explain that none of us had done it based on the confiscated guns. Still, due process had to be done, and we were granted a Lawyer for our group trial.

Our Boss posted bail for us in the interim so we could avoid having our asses beaten or legitimately killing people in prison and have another thing to keep us in a cell. Nice of him, considering the circumstances. Something did not sit right with me, though.

There were two suspects in his compound, but as some may recall, we have one person who worked with our Boss to protect a kid. One person from a rival gang was found innocent, and lastly, there is a chance whoever was on the news last chapter is within our jurisdiction despite the fact he is wanted in two States and could have done it. Unlikely, but not impossible. Until we are cleared of charges, any evidence we might find of other unsolved cases would likely be thrown out, so we saw it as a break from our usual work. We sure needed it.

Sadly, like all vacations, it felt too short for us as we were served in court within the standard time frame.

Judge Accurate was on the case, and our defense attorney was, ironically enough, Silvester Shields. The prosecution was Samantha Stockade.

"All parties have been-

"Lailah, what?

"How?

"Ahem, never mind, all parties have been sworn in, and then we shall proceed with Furry Investigation Department 310 Vs. the State of California."

Samantha Stockade began her opening statement, "People of the jury, the evidence presented today collected by the San Francisco Police Department will show that these cretins killed a veteran engineer in cold blood."

Silvester Shields responded, "And I say the evidence will show none of these respectable mystery-solving geniuses had done anything to kill Thaddius Yu."

Judge Accurate nodded, "Very well, let us proceed."

Exhibit A; the guns found on their person the day the crime occurred and all bullets in them.

Exhibit B The autopsy report and forensic analysis of the body by a different Investigation team

Exhibit C is the bullet found inside Thaddius Yu's body. Exhibit D shows the Police interrogation before them requesting their right to an attorney and afterward.

Lastly, there was Exhibit E, the recording of the private discussion with Thaddius Yu courtesy of Leonard.

Samantha continued, "Perhaps the most damning evidence here is Exhibit C, the bullet found in the victim.

"It matches the guns they all used perfectly, and thus they must have done it.

"They were found on the scene and had reason to be there, as Exhibit D suggests."

Silvester retorted, "I say Exhibit D disproves Exhibit A and C.

"When they were taken in for questioning, all their guns were full.

"If we look at Exhibit A closely, they have an entire set of new rounds inside the guns.

"There are no traces they had ever even tested them.

"To elaborate, we have none other than their Boss, Bill Benson, to testify for them here.

Bill Benson took the witness stand.

"Mr. Benson, will you kindly tell the courts why these suspects were on Alcatraz Island on the day of the murder?"

"Gladly. I served alongside some good and some bad guys when I was in the army.

"And among the more ruthless was Thaddius Yu.

"We had up to this point at one unsolved case file involving unregistered guns and a missing person who was investigated and dismissed.

"While he did not serve on the front lines and his roles were more in making weapons and sending them out, his attitude was as fierce as any soldier.

"We had reason to believe he could have had something to do with it. I knew him to be a talented engineer of weapons, including tanks. He could have gotten around the registration law for ranged weapons if he had made them.

"Moreover, I gathered from doing a little investigative work that he used to be a part of the Heaven's Demons motorcycle gang.

"He had left amid the mistrust when many had entered the witness protection program.

"So, it is entirely possible one of them, or perhaps a rival gang, was behind it, but that is neither here nor there as far as this case is concerned.

"The point is I gave them those guns and a specific number of rounds and magazines, which the evidence shows they spent not a single bullet even after they saw him die.

"Thus, it was not them who shot Thaddius Yu."

"That will do, Mr. Benson.

"So, you see, they had a reason to be there. They were provided with ammunition for their weapons, and their guns were confirmed unused by the recording and the person testifying today.

"While the bullet may have matched the ones they would use in their gun, these weapons are not significantly different from an earth-made handgun and thus could use the same ammo theoretically."

"But what about the Autopsy report and the forensic analysis report?

"The bullet was from a gun they had, and they could have done the deed."

"That is also untrue.

"While the bullet looked like one they had for their weapons, the shot was traced back to an earth-made handgun belonging to Henry Skins.

"Henry Skins, as some may or may not know, is very much deceased.

"Because of that, I would posit that my clients are innocent. "Which means someone has been following their work long enough to know where to be and when.

"Someone must have come upon their weapons before or after their deaths.

"Absent that it would have to be someone who inherited the items or whose business it is to decide where the deceased's possessions go.

"Security would have been too tight on the items for someone to waltz in and grab someone's weapon undetected.

"Possibilities to theft would require stealth training or knowledge of police procedures or perhaps connections to those on the inside."

"What about someone he knew who he frequently hung out with?

"I find things can quickly go missing when fake friends are around.

"Or what if they use similar items?

"Someone else could have thought it was theirs and taken it in error."

"An interesting theory, but that does not answer the question of what motive that same person would have to go and kill their friend.

"Or get it in hands that would."

Judge Accurate chimed in, "I think we are getting off track.

"The question here is not whether or not someone else did the deed, but did these here do it or have any motive to do it?"

Samantha nodded, "The defense would say they would not, but none of us were there to see what was said."

Silvester seemed to agree, "Maybe not see, but that is where I remind you of Exhibit E, the recording of the discussion between them from a hidden recorder Leonard cleverly brought with him."

The recording played with everything that was said after they went in private.

"So, you see my clients based on the exchange there, and you could not hear a bullet fired yet panicked movements and dialog to suggest someone has been hit, whoever did this had a silencer.

"None of the weapons collected into evidence here had one.

"Thus, they could not have used them to commit the crime, and they had no other items on their person that could have done it."

"This is hearsay.

"They could have moved around for several reasons."

"The time stamps of the audio log and the estimated time of death from the forensic lab match perfectly."

"But they agreed to keep this guy's actions a secret and even join up with him."

"Knowing what sort of a dangerous and unpredictable man he was according to their limited information, I would venture to say they did it out of self-preservation instinct.

"For all they knew, he could have had all sorts of traps or means to force their cooperation, and thus they were likely under duress."

"I-they-I have nothing evidentiary.

"However, I humbly ask the Jury to consider the precedent of letting these people go.

"They work on cases for several police forces, and letting them go could lead to similar groups acting as if they can do whatever they want, and the law need not apply to them."

"With that, let us move on to closing statements."

"As I said, these people were found at the crime scene with weapons that matched the crime and the last ones seen with them.

"Even if we can say they did not kill the man, would the two men held captive when they were found not constitute kidnapping or co-conspiracy?"

"And I say they did what they could with the unknown circumstances and thus should not be deemed guilty of a murder they did not do.

"The kidnapping part ought to be dismissed as well since, on the audio log, the man they spoke to kept them there instead of serving time with other inmates who would have killed them.

"He was simultaneously letting them work for him.

"Not only that, but we had no clue what danger they would have been in had they refused his offer."

The Jury went back and deliberated.

Their verdict was "not guilty" because of insufficient evidence to prove their guilt beyond a shadow of a doubt and possible duress.

With that Judge Accurate saw, us free to resume our work. I enjoyed the break from the insanity but was relieved to be off the hook and even more satisfied to see the anger in Ms. Stockade's eyes.

"You! One day I will break you."

I'm not going to lie. It shook us all up being on trial like this. To think this is what our work puts so many through, whether innocent or not. You may be wondering what became of the suspects we found. Well, that is where this gets interesting. We weren't the only ones on trial today. Since this story only covers what my team or I saw, we later found that Mr. Coy was not guilty of fleeing prosecution because of his abduction but guilty of providing weapons to underage people and Manslaughter. However, the courts deducted his time presumably caged on Alcatraz Island from his sentence. The prosecution tried to pin him with first-degree murder on account of the fact he may have known the kids would fight over the one weapon he gifted them and for leading them to a place near the man's home enough to kill him, but there was insufficient evidence to convict him of that. Since it could not be considered conclusive whether the ones who meant to shoot the gun or the ones trying to stop them ended up firing the shot and being minors under 12 could not be faced with juvenile hall, but they did have their weapons confiscated.

Their adoptive mother was still in jail. The court appointed a guardian to take her place following her trial. Little did we know we were about to stumble upon something that could change everything. Though Mr. Mc Coy was now in jail for a reduced sentence, the case we worked on remained before the interruption by being arrested. Who poisoned Theodore Journeyman? The other guy supposedly held at the compound we know as Assn seemed the obvious suspect, given he does jobs for the government, or so Thaddius said, though I have to wonder who all has been lying to me up to now and what were the lies.

While we were on trial, a breakthrough happened in the case. One might remember Thaddius Yu had gotten in with the Heaven's Demons at one point. Well, shockingly, they were not to blame for the caper we went to investigate. Though the trial had gone cold, Proxy seemed to have found some suspicious activities of one online called "Victor Vindicator." From what he saw by following threads and IP address information, a user perused a front door listing for a medicine that will cure depression for those without health insurance. He then agreed to make a deal in San Pedro in a back alley near the electrical place we first went. If the IP address was traced correctly, perhaps, someone in the firm did it—someone he trusted. I sent in Leonard Rudderbeaut as he would better fish out the lies.

This was what he found in his logs and recordings.

Logically the first place to interrogate would be the one closest to him, so I, Leonard Rudderbeaut, took it upon myself to meet with his son first.

"So, Matthias Journeyman, I presume?"

"The very same.

"You already interrogated me once about my dad.

"What more could you need to know?"

"Some new evidence has come to light since our investigation was put on hold.

"It would seem a drug deal occurred less than five days before your dad's death."

"Okay... so what does that have to do with me?"

"Does the screen name Victor Vindicator ring a bell?"

He suddenly seemed shocked, as if he knew something.

"H-Him... he...I..."

"Go on, spill it.

"Need I remind you that failing to divulge what you know could render obstruction of justice charges, and you could serve time regardless of if you were in on a conspiracy to murder?"

"Okay... I will tell you everything I know.

"I knew that as widely successful as my dad was, he always seemed discontented.

"There would be days I could not even get him to wake up for work which made it difficult to get new clients on board for work to be done.

"While, as a company, we could get prescription drugs with a small copay and have him see a psychiatrist, the prescribed drugs only seemed to make him more dormant and less active.

"I was getting desperate for anything that could help him."

"So, you went online as Victor Vindicator and bought pills you thought would help him?"

"N-No... I asked another team member Jerry Gerbil to see what he could find out using the good old internet.

"He went to Front Page and contacted a Victor Vindicator.

"It was a screen name, so we thought little of it.

"I mean, who doesn't go online with an alias?

"Jerry's is Petfood12345."

"That is about all the questions, then.

"Can you bring in Jerry?"

Sounds of movement and seating are heard on the tape.

"Hello, I am Jerry."

"So, your leader tells me he sent you on an errand to get some medicine?"

"Y-Yeah..."

"Well, did you know what those pills you gave his dad was?"

"N-No, the bottle had no label since it was well not on the main market, but very effective."

"If by effective you mean they make their victims as dead outside as they feel inside, then yes!"

Jerry is trembling now, barely able to keep his words.

"I am s-sorry... I did not know..."

"Do you have a description of what the guy looked like?"

"He appeared to be some mutant.

"He was neither human nor animal.

"Perhaps he was a genetic experiment?"

"Oh?"

"Yeah, I heard rumors in addition to experimental gender transitioning procedures, there are also species ones.

"The latter is perhaps a bit less studied, especially with the current political climate."

"Well, that does narrow it down quite a bit.

"Thank you, you have been accommodating."

The recording finished, and I wondered what sort of place might engineer a way for humans to turn into animals. Not like HIPPA laws would allow me to get information on their patients, so we need to prepare a sting operation to get this one in custody. I made the required calls to our local department, and we went back to Front Page and looked up offerings under the Victor Vindicator. He does not cover his tracks well for one who dabbles in drugs. Maybe he does not know the drugs were used to kill someone yet. It did not break the news either, or he is ready with a defense for all this.

Sure enough, the sting was a success.

In the interrogation room

"So, Victor Vindicator, I presume?

"Real name Victor Vanguard?

"My, you look like a mess, more so than the ones we usually get into this room."

"..."

"A silent one, eh?

"Well, I think you know why you are here.

"A man with depression died because of the drugs you sold his employee.

"What have you to say to that?"

"I would like to speak with an attorney and have them present."

Questioning ceased, and an attorney was brought in Carole Charter.

"My client says that any drug can be overdosed and lead to death, and there was nothing specific about the drugs that would have been fatal. Moreover, they are used medicinally for a certain STD."

"Then we have you selling drugs without a license and thus trafficking, possessing drugs, and possibly manslaughter."

"My client reasonably thought these drugs, if used appropriately, would help a condition."

"Then why were there no instructions for use on the bottle?"

"My client told them not to exceed a single pill to test the effects before risking an increase in dose."

"If it is not in writing, I fail to see how you can prove that."

"Be that as it may, he had no other source of income.

"Who would hire someone who mutated themselves into whatever that is save for illegal trades?"

"Poverty is not a defense for murder.

"Theft maybe, but murder, no."

"He just wanted to be furry like one of you but could not afford the experimental procedures.

"He would do anything to help his species dysphoria."

"Again, that does not absolve him from what he has purportedly done."

"We have nothing further, so we will wait for a trial."

With that, the questioning went nowhere else, and as per the law, we could only hold them for questioning for so long once an attorney was present.

Then came the day of the trial.

Judge Accurate was presiding.

"We shall now hear the case of Victor Vanguard VS The State of California. Opening statements, please."

Ian Imprison was the prosecutor; no surprise, Carol Charter was the defense attorney.

"We have a case of illicit sale of drugs used to commit murder.

"Let us not be persuaded by the fact this monster wanted to be one of those furry things and focus on the cold hard facts!"

"And I say it is a case of our racist and unaccepting system refusing to give a man with a dream a chance to be what he always wanted without resorting to illicit trades.

"The man did not know the drugs he sold were inherently poisonous beyond that of other prescription drugs.

"He questioned if the hype around their illicit nature was overblown, much like catnip or marijuana.

"We are in no way attempting to dispute drugs were sold here, but that he should not be considered a manslaughter perpetrator.

"The intent was lacking."

Then came the evidence

Ian Imprison kicked it off, "I bring to your attention Exhibit A, the Drugs found on the person at the crime scene.

"Exhibit B, the conversation between the two on an instant messenger, the trade's time and place.

"Exhibit C the autopsy and forensic findings that indeed drugs matching exhibit A were used in the death of Theodore Journeyman."

"For context to how it all went down, Exhibit D The interrogation tapes."

Judge Accurate nodded, "Proceed."

"Take a look at the pill bottle.

"There are no written instructions on how to safely use the product, even if we ignore that it is demonstrably an illicit substance with few exceptions.

"It brings to question what sort of clients this... thing intended to sell drugs.

"How do we know he informed anyone how to use the substances? Even if we ignored the illegality of his operation, there are no instructions?"

"A person who is not a pharmacist may not have the supplies to print a bottle label.

"Especially if they run on a shoestring profit margin and have to evade law enforcement that may be patrolling."

"And how about the conversation between him and the buyer indicated they knew what they were dealing with substance-wise?

"A substance that a reasonable person should know these were inherently dangerous?"

"Prescription drugs were ineffective with the depression the late Theodore Journeyman suffered.

"It seems both intended to try something with unknown medicinal properties and see if it works."

"Why did they not just use MDMA then or Ecstasy?

"The dealer was not afraid to operate illegally."

"Those drugs aren't as easily obtained.

"With Thallium having been prescribed to those with Syphilis, it is much more likely to find someone who might have it."

"And lastly, we should play the interrogation tapes as the autopsy, and the forensic report doesn't need much explaining.

"It says exactly what I am that the man died from Thallium poisoning from this freak show!"

The tapes played. The Jury seemed in tears that this man just wanted to be something other than what he was born.

"So, you see my client, to help fund this experimental procedure, had to turn to a life of crime.

"No one else would have kept him on their payroll if they knew he was transitioning.

"Though discrimination is illegal, companies have managers who know how to make nonsense excuses to dismiss someone for anything.

"If this man made any mistakes that demonstrably cost the company a single red cent, proving wrongful termination is next to impossible."

"What about furry-run firms?

"Surely one of them would have been sympathetic to his plight and let him in?"

"Can you name a single firm like that besides the detective agency that was on trial recently or their sibling companies?"

"No, but surely if their collective just collaborated, they could pull together the resources to do it."

"And then what?

"Racists come knocking with burning stakes and hammer and tails logos and destroy all they worked for?"

"That is a bunch of malarky and beyond the facts in this case.

To bring some sense to this, I call my expert toxicologist Tanner Toxic to the stand."

Tanner Toxic took the stand and was sworn in.

"Tanner tell me, is the medicinal claims behind Thallium accurate, precisely the kind sold in this case?

"Or does its reputation of the poisoner's poison hold?"

"Well, amid the forensic reports you submitted to evidence, you will find I had personally analyzed the pills and body in question for the toxicology report.

"I can confirm that the pills given were diluted enough that a reasonable person could have taken one and been okay.

"Trouble is with conditions like depression. It is not unheard of for people to commit suicide by drug overdose.

"Drug overdose could have happened with nearly any prescription or over-the-counter drug.

"Thallium, however, requires fewer pills to achieve that, which is part of why it is only available by prescription under particular circumstances.

"So, I do not deny that it was reckless to be selling it on the black market, but at some level, it is the responsibility of the user to regulate their use."

"That will do, Mr. Toxic.

"So, you see, people of the Jury, a reasonable person would have known better than to sell these drugs to someone at risk for overdosing."

"Be that as it may, neither your expert nor physical evidence has demonstrated intent to kill someone.

"You also failed to demonstrate that the substance given could not have been used safely or that my client did not know it could be used safely or had any motive to kill the man.

"Thus, to consider this manslaughter even involuntarily is pretty weak."

The Judge seemed impatient, "Are there any more witnesses to call, or are we about ready to wrap this up?"

"No one, your honor."

"Very well, let us wrap this up with closing statements."

"So, you see, people of the Jury, while the evidence for Manslaughter is questionable, no one can dispute he illegally sold drugs.

"Someone died because of it, and I say we lock him up!"

"And I say we show him mercy as he did his best to make it in this world.

"He tried to treat his dysphoria, and I do not expect him to be absolved of the crimes brought before him fully.

"We can offer him the tools to go on the good path and reach his goals."

The Jury reached a tearful verdict.

"We find the defendant innocent of manslaughter charges but guilty of drug trafficking and possession."

Judge Accurate nodded, "Because it seems like the motive for the crime was a mental condition, I am going to give it the minimum sentence of 5 years in prison.

"I could give 20 years because of the injury involved or death.

However, the lack of intent to kill suggests they still have a chance.

"During the five-year sentence, I will allow them to have an education in Entrepreneurship and perhaps pharmaceuticals if that is their passion.

"I would like to see this one's life turned around and be an example of what one can become if their resolve is steadfast.

"We are adjourned!"

With the gavel bang, the defendant was taken to a minimum-security prison with vocational programs.

And our chapter is reaching its end, but before it does this, I would be remiss to forget to tell you while I was observing this trial, a separate one was held for Jerry on the same facts and evidence. There were still enough pills and copies of the same evidence to hold both trials simultaneously. He got charged with Possession and illicit purchase of drugs and got five years as well for giving the drugs to the one who died. He also got an extra year for Involuntary Manslaughter, which was pretty light since he intended to help the man. The only other illegal act was buying drugs off the black market. He had been the one to give the pills to the man personally, so there was slightly more liability on him than the seller. Moreover, he could have destroyed the drugs since he did not depend on them for income.

With that, we close this chapter with not 2 but 4 trials, of which we saw only two, and each had a related one happening simultaneously. Thus, it was a battle of the trials scenario that happened twice.

CHAPTER 12

HOLIDAY HAVOC

It is all Fun and Games

After a lengthy and well-orchestrated set of cases, including one about us, Winter and the holidays were on, namely, Chanukah at this point, as it usually begins before Christmas. In spirit, Bill Benson invited us to his mansion for a dinner party, and as a team, we decided to take him up on it. So up Palos Verdes Hill, we went to a massive home overlooking the ocean, and you could see Catalina Island from up there.

"Ah, what a beautiful place to host a party."

"I am glad you think so, Lailah.

"I think you will find this place is a testament to hard work paying off.

"I have been in this business a long time.

"If I were you, I would consider buying a few rental properties.

"Get three solid ones, and someday you will not have to work another day."

"Then why do you still work?"

"Because though I could have retired a decade ago, our firm work holds too much meaning.

"Especially as tensions rise between Furries and humans."

"Good to have work you enjoy, I suppose.

"Me, I am unsure lately.

"Things have kind of been weird."

"Oh, how so?"

"Well, a while back, I fell asleep in front of my TV and had strangely vivid nightmares.

"It was like I was peering into another reality created by a writer who knows nothing about subtlety in creating a horror setting."

"Oh, you mean like when you dream of kids' show suddenly turning into a bad work of a fictional lost episode?"

I looked at him, slightly surprised. "Exactly that."

"Yeah, I get those too periodically, but hey, dreams are dreams, and until I see scythe cat in my house, I am not inclined to worry about it."

"Maybe not Scythe cat specifically, but I am told dreams can be warnings of events to come sometimes if one analyzes them correctly."

"Sounds superstitious to me, but hey, let's raise a glass to a good Y-"

Suddenly the lights flashed, and it was just Bill Benson sitting at the table and me. He seemed most annoyed and on guard, as would be expected if someone crashed their party.

"What is the meaning of this?"

"I do not know, but this looks bad."

A note was on the table and read,

If you are reading this, then consider it game on.

To unlock the next door, remember well the cases you worked on. Each holds a clue to your escape.

"Is this that mystery game you spoke of on your vacation?"

"It would seem, so whoever devised this must have intimate knowledge of how we think and work as a team, but how did they gain control of your home?"

"No clue.

"Proxy Foxy is supposed to be in charge of my security systems."

We heard a muffled scream for help near us.

We go to the flailing box and open it to find Proxy inside and untie him.

"Mr. Benson, it is awful the one I had been tracking...They..."

"Calm down.

"We will get out of this together."

He nodded as we searched about the place and saw some hospital items strewn about, including some of the plush toys Lailah used to give to patients before she became a Forensic Anthropologist.

"These toys seem familiar... but what could they mean?"

"Lailah, think hard... in your last job, did anyone, and I mean anyone, hate you or get offended by anything you gave them?"

"Not that I remember.

"However, I do remember a guy who looked like Adam volunteered briefly when he was, I want to say, 4.

"It was several months before the fall of the preschool, and I gave him a glow-in-the-dark teddy bear."

Proxy searched the one glow-in-the-dark teddy bear amongst the lot of them.

"Aha! There is a note!"

Place bear into the arms of the child who deserves it.

A light shined on some statues, one of which looked like Adam. After putting two and two together, I placed it in the Adam statue's arms, and a scythe came down and landed in its arms as it still held the plush, and the door opened. We saw Adam hanging in a cage above the room, scared as it swung around, which would be a perpetual hell to anyone afraid of heights.

"Please, I am not ready to die yet!"

Seeing how much Adam had grown when I last saw him was shocking. Then I thought about the scythe.

"How does someone even have that kind of a trap?"

Bill explained, "That cage was meant to lock up intruders till the police could come, and I had never seen those statues before."

I examined the cage and the scythe, "Maybe we could cut down the cage with that scythe that dropped. Those chains do not look like they are particularly resistant to it."

Proxy read the following note.

Do not use the scythe that dropped to cut down the cage or do.

Cats always land on their feet, but does it hurt?

To safely lower the crank, consider who you took to the bank.

Proxy looked at us, "Hmm, a bit premature to ask, but if the last case's answer had to do with the first major case you worked on, could there be a theme to the expected answers?"

I remembered the first case I worked on, "It is possible.

"I know that the first case I worked on involved Adam."

"My team and the police determined early on he was unlikely as a suspect to have done it.

"The same thing happened with Neko in the case after that."

We searched around to find a hat next to a picture of a field then we found a kid's playset that looked like an orphan house.

"Get me down from here already!"

"Consider who we took to the bank... wait, if we took it there.

"That means something will happen, so maybe if we put the clues that spell out Hatfield and put them next to the orphans on the table, but what is missing?

"The gun!"

We looked around, found a toy gun, and put it on the table next to the other two items. The cage came down slowly, and Bill Benson opened the cell, and the crying cat person hugged me and purred.

"T-thank you for rescuing me..."

He quickly ran for the back room and grabbed the plush bear and scythe.

"Weird as it sounds, these just feel right to hold."

"You're scaring me, Adam."

"How?"

"Dreams..."

"Oh..."

We proceeded on and saw the door had locked a note nearby.

Though you unlocked the cage and freed the cat boy, there is just one more thing to open the door. Who was the suspect in the case who was dismissed without trial?

We saw a plush cat with yellowish fur and blue eyes. We put it with the other items, and the door opened. In the next room, we found the same blond-haired, blue-eyed cat boy tinkering with some machinery.

"Neko! Did you do this?"

"Do what?"

"Setup this mystery game?"

"Mystery game? I woke up here too with no memory of how I ended up here, so I have been building toys out of boredom."

"Well, like it or not, someone took inspiration from your escape room and hacked into Bill Benson's security systems.

"Someone is toying with us like we paid to be toyed with in your place."

"Well, I do not know any more about your cases than the TV shows me."

Adam looked at me confidently, "I think I can solve this one.

"The third major News Broadcast case you were in involved the one who killed my parents."

He fervently searched the room to find a family doll house. He put the parents in their bed and an object on them as if to indicate they had been hit and tied the two sister dolls around a piece of parachute string, and sure enough, a paper dropped.

Good job, you figured it out, but just one piece is missing. Who did it?

We saw a light shine on three statues in the room one that looked like Lily Lockup, one that looked like Adam, and another that could not be identified readily as a generic men's room man.

Following the prompt, Bill Benson surprisingly put the scythe Adam was holding into the arms of the strange statue, and the room opened.

"I knew something seemed fishy about Lily Lockups' case."

In the next room, we found a bunch of letters, an electric chair model, a switch, Lily Lockup, Silvester Shields, and Kang Roo. Above the three of them was a spike ceiling. Upon pulling a note from its hanging place, the door locked behind us, and the roof lowered slowly.

There is not much time.

Legal proceedings take lots of it.

The death penalty is even longer.

One of you must sit in the chair of death.

It will not kill you, but it should satisfy the anger one of you holds for all the others.

It makes no difference to me who sits in the chair.

One of you is about to get a massive dose of electroshock therapy to help with your

insanity.

It was what Adam wanted in his letters to you, Lailah."

Lily Lockup was tied up, as was Silvester Shields.

Adam smiled a bit, "If we weren't about to get crushed by spikes, I would say Lily could use it for her hate of my kind, but it is clear what must happen."

He walked right for the electric chair.

I called after him, "Adam, don't!

"We do not know if the person who kept us here is lying.

"You could die here!"

"I will join my parents if I do, plus I doubt any of you will volunteer to test it.

"Moreover, electroshock therapy was discredited, so no matter who it is will not likely be improved by it any."

Adam gave my face a comforting lick as he went over to the chair and sat in it, taking the electric shock to save us all. His screams of agony and fear were enough to make any cat owner cry. His body convulsed in periodic motions and directions.

When he did not move, I felt tears well in my eyes, but the spikes stopped just 10 feet above our heads and retracted back up as the shock concluded. It had been about 100 feet up before the touching decision and subsequent shock. I felt the weight of what he had done take over me, and Bill tried to comfort me.

"Lailah... I am sorry..."

"No need, I will be fine."

Proxy interjected, "But..."

"I said it was fine, and we had to go.

"I just hope Adam's soul is at peace."

I then heard a cough.

"He's alive?"

I ran up and hugged him, which in retrospect, was dumb since he had just been subject to an electric shock, and I immediately felt the consequences of that and let out pained yelps of my own as my body convulsed around as he did prior.

The cat boy coughed and laughed, "You probably don't need me to say it, but until the electricity is discharged from me, you may need to use rubber gloves and a rubber suit when interacting with me.

"Also, keep me away from water since it conducts electricity."

"You were so brave taking that when you could have instead subjected anyone to it."

"None of them did it if we are to believe the last clue, so a man on the path of revenge must dig two graves.

"Presumably, the second grave is for the one who wanted revenge.

"Because the path to revenge spells ruin for all who walk it."

"I am impressed they are teaching deeper stuff than I was growing up."

"Schools no longer teach philosophy, just practical skills to get jobs.

"I read that more out of personal interest in a library before some human children wanted to pet me because I look like a housecat.

"It did not seem to matter to them that I am anthropomorphic."

"Glad to know not all humans hate Furries."

"Yeah, it varies a lot.

"Sadly, places, where crimes like these happen tend to be hotbeds for racism while areas more inclusive tend to be just the opposite.

"Nevertheless, we must proceed as I never asked to be an uninvited guest here any more than anyone else."

We freed Lily, Silvester, and Kang.

"Can't believe I got saved by that cat boy, and he is still alive, damn it all!

"I have half a mind to strangle him here, and who would prove I done it?"

Silvester sighed, "This is not the time, Lily.

"We are all stuck here together and must find our way out.

"Otherwise, we will eventually run out of food and water and die of dehydration or starvation.

"Unless you fancy, we go the Donnor Party route."

Kang Roo bounced around excitedly at being freed, not seeming particularly perturbed by the dialog around him. I envy a spirit like that, especially in such dire circumstances as these.

In the next room, we found Alan Saikumar Silverstein-Nakiah, or alias Assn the Assassin, milling about, looking for a way out of here.

"I should have known this was a trap."

"What was?"

"I was sent to investigate a Mr. Benson, and when I checked the address, it did not add up, and before I knew it, I passed out.

"If I had to guess, they must have used chloroform gas in the room they led me into."

I looked around to see if anything seemed amiss, and there appeared to be a couple of toy houses stacked next to each other and some target dummies. There was a note inside.

One among you was not served justice.

The system itself protects the guilty and frames the innocent.

Held to be a government patsy as it pursues its more nefarious goals, the public never knows.

I offer a chance to right the wrong here and now.

I know he is a skilled assassin, but they cannot plan for everything.

Otherwise, I would not have captured him.

Solve this room's puzzle and subject him to the justice he deserves.

Alan looked around, "So this is how it ends, eh?

"If you solve this room, I die. If you don't, we are stuck here forever."

I chimed in, "Or so he would have us believe.

"I am slightly skeptical after Adam survived the electric chair."

"Well, I spent most of my life captive working for the government, and frankly, I am sick of it.

"I never thought the witness protection program could be worse than regular jail.

"So do it solve the puzzle and put me out of my misery."

"Well, what do you know of the case you almost got put away for?"

"I was there to investigate a person of interest.

"As you already know, I was shot at when passively investigating.

"I was found not guilty by self-defense, but I killed them.

"Though the evidence was somewhat dubious, I had been sent there on suspicion they might be up to the illegal activity.

"If I caught them conspiring to do anything, I would take them out with lethal or non-lethal force as appropriate.

"Since I did not have guns when I came to their place, and they did, proving self-defense was easy."

"There's got to be another clue to this..."

It was then we noticed the judge's stand and mock court setup.

"Or maybe the intent was not to kill you but symbolically serve you the sentence you should have got in the mind of whoever designed this place."

Kang Roo took the judge's stand, and Lily and Silvester took their usual roles as we recreated the trial. The rest of us played jury except me, who supposedly had the evidence. When all was said and done, the jury found Alan guilty, and upon doing so, Kang Roo sentenced him to death row, where he would await proper execution for cold-blooded murder. None of us saw a spike coming from under Alan's defendant chair and impaled him through his crotch to his head.

Adam cringed seeing this and trembled a bit. I put on rubber gloves and pat him, assuming he was still electrically charged. He purred and seemed to calm down.

The door opened, and though we were more or less shaken by what we saw, we proceeded slowly.

Inside was Linus Lynx, Kit Kit, Kit Kat, and an unidentified kid hugging a kitten. We also had the

Duke of Earl Street, "Hunter."

None of these people even killed anyone. Why are they here? Well, except Linus, maybe.

Linus gave me a note.

Justice is blind and unbiased, yet what do all these you freed have in common?

"Common hmm..."

Kit Kit said, "You thought we might have killed someone a rich kid accidentally killed."

Hunter thought momentarily and spoke, "I was suspected often of stealing things though never charged for it."

The unidentified kid spoke, "I am Isaac, and I love to hug animals. I am, however, visiting from my home country Israel."

"Did you get up to any antics while in Israel or here?"

"Um, I lost my Passport when I wound up here."

"So, from a very loose sense, everyone we freed could be a suspect of a different crime, but what does that mean for opening the next door?"

"Wait, justice is blind..."

I looked around and found a box of blindfolds.

"Maybe putting these blindfolds on will solve the room."

We all put on the blindfolds and felt our way to the door, which opened to our touch.

Yet another locked room, but this time we found Axel Flask and Herbert Harbinger XIV.

Axel Flask seemed to catch on with what we were doing together.

"Becoming a real reunion now, is it not?"

"But where are PI Patrick, Cat Sleuth, and Leonard Rudderbeaut?"

Bill Benson said, "Don't know, but so far, we found everyone who did not die in our cases except them."

Herbert was dead silent, unsure what to make of all of this.

Neko asked, "Do you think one of them may have set this up?"

I replied, "Maybe Leonard or Cat since they both seem to like puzzles, but what about Sofer?"

"Nah, I may not know Sofer well, but he does not strike me as being particularly handy with technology as much as words."

Kit Kat said, "Well, it could not have been us.

"What kind of idiot would become part of their trap like this?"

I replied, "Don't know, but this is all so weird. How could anyone have planned something elaborate like this and set up so many puzzles behind Benson's back?

"It does not make sense."

Neko laughed, "If I survive this, I will choose a more peaceful career path.

"Maybe I could make a golf game where instead of aiming for holes, you aim for targets instead.

"And have cameras track the ball's movement to simulate the play.

"I could call it 'Switch Golf' because you could readily switch between different game modes if you got tired of one."

Adam chuckled, "Who would pay money to play practice golf?"

Neko shrugged, "People pay money to sing in karaoke booths or buy alcohol for free karaoke on stage.

"If alcohol is involved, anything could be a profitable idea."

Adam chuckled, "Good luck with that.

"I would instead invent a way for people to express their least popular opinions nonviolently and find like-minded individuals.

"I would call it 'Cat Box' and call the submissions people made on the site 'Scat Posts.'

"Then implement a messaging feature to allow people who connect to exchange information and meet up if the distance is doable.

"Unlike a dating site, I would want people to come together around mutual dislikes and likes rather than superficial things like pictures of each other.

"Then even if they catfish one another, a friendship can be made at least assuming the likes and dislikes were true."

Neko laughed, "And that would make the world a better place. How?"

Adam remarked, "It wouldn't, but sometimes mutual hate breeds stronger connections than likes.

"'The enemy of my enemy is my friend,' as they say."

Kit Kit said, “If possible, I would enjoy operating an outdoor barbeque hibachi style or fresh-caught fish restaurant offering sushi and cooked fish options.”

Kit Kat nodded, “We could also make a sort of cooking show, maybe a series of them.

“One I think would be particularly niche is ‘Camp Kit Cooking’ or ‘What does the fox bake?’

“We could teach tv audiences how to make delicious and wholesome food from naturally occurring sources around them as well as delicacies involving things they bring from home that can be made using camping appliances.”

Adam mused, “Sounds like it could be big in the future, but I am doubtful it would catch on now any more than me making a rock band with Neko and Isaac. If we did, though, we would call it ‘Infinite Death’ and do a mix of alternative rock and metal-style music. Maybe found our radio station.”

Neko said, “Yeah, and we could form an intergalactic TV network known as 'Neko TV.'"

“It would soon expand to become its intergalactic cable and streaming company.”

Adam said, “Yeah, and I would read internet copy and paste stories and horror stories, including ones I write, and visually act out stories that are scary to viewers.

“We should also let viewers call in with suggestions on how to make our shows more interesting so that we can evolve.”

While Adam, Neko, Kit Kit, Kit Kat, and Isaac mused about their futures, I was focused on only one thing. We were finding our way out.

The next note clue was as follows:

The Son was punished for the wishes of the Father.

The Father loved the game, but the Son did not.

Judaism does not believe in original Sin, but Christianity does.

Separate the Father from the Son to reveal the Sin.

With the help of the others in the room, we lifted the statue of the Son off of the Father, and sure enough, the Hebrew letter Sin revealed the next clue.

Good job.

The sins of the Father are not the sins of the Son.

You think the room is over, but it is only just begun.

To unlock the door, consider the power of four.

Bill Benson looked at me curiously as he observed how I went about solving this room but said nothing.

"Four.

"I, Cat, Leonard, and Patrick each have a different specialty.

"Patrick seems good at visual puzzles, while I excel at words.

"Cat seems to be our logician, and Leonard our numbers guy.

"Power of 4..."

I counted the number of people in the room.

There are 16 of us and two doors. If we all try to pry the door open, it would be 2 to the power of 4 or 16 people.

I found some rope in the room, tied it to the door handle, and each of us pulled on it like a game of tug of war. A number lit up on the screen above the door and read "16."

Best I could figure, sensors beneath the ground or on the door calculated how many of us were trying to pry open the door to arrive at that number. Either way, the door opened after that, and we proceeded.

In the next room, I found Samantha Stockade, Judge Accurate, Judge Monsoon, Kevin Key, and Simon Southsea in one corner. Cait Smith, Orvan Plaid, and Mr. Mc Coy are in the second corner. Mathias Journeyman, Jerry Gerbil, Victor Vindicator, Tanner Toxic in a third corner. Carole Charter, Ian Imprison, Leonard Rudder-Beaut, the orphans Lily Lockup cared for, and Cat Sleuth in the center of the room. Yeah, we had freed all who were stuck here. Among them were the gang leaders of Claws, Paws, and Heavens Demons and any members they had besides ones in court cases, Former Mayor Money Bags members of Hammer and Nails, Sofer, and PI Patrick.

This time it seemed like we had hit a dead end, though—no way forward or back.

I shouted, "Well, we found everyone, but where is the exit?

"Are there any more clues?"

Suddenly PI Patrick got up and put on the most sinister smile I had ever seen. He walked over to a wall and knocked on it to be lowered into an escape rocket. Then, before we could stop him, Patrick hit a button. A wall rose in front of us, separating our portion of the room from the one he was in. He blasted off, and a video monitor came out with his face on it.

"Well, isn't this nice?

"The gangs all here, I see, or are they?

"As a reward for solving these puzzles, I have sent evidence to forgive the people we locked away till now as none of them had a clue. "However, as Lailah suggested at the dinner table, I have fled the Country.

"You just saw me take off in that rocket.

"The United States and Russia have always been old foes, so I doubt I will not be disengaged from the States.

"Before I reveal why I did this, I ask you a series of questions.

"Who was it that was involved in nearly all of your cases?

"Who was that one you immediately dismissed as impossible from the get-go?

"Someone you knew a long time and swore on your life could never be capable of any of this?"

I thought for a moment as a microphone came down.

"PI Patrick?"

"Why, why would you do this?

"We gave you a place to be when everyone else left you.

"You had a job and reason to continue.

"Sure, I made jokes about you periodically, like how you could not find your way out of a cardboard box, but I never meant it literally."

"That's right!

"'I couldn't find my way out of a cardboard box.'"

"I was joking.

"You did not have to take it to heart."

"That is not it at all.

"This entire time, did you never once find it fishy one as incompetent and needing help could ever get to be a PI?

"How the answers always went under my nose until... wham!

"A clue I swore I did not find is there!"

"How did you manipulate all these people to do your bidding?"

"Simple, I convinced Mr. Hatfield he could save a lot of money by firing his IT crew, outsourcing them to India, and getting just as good a service.

"That made Mr. Mc Coy want him dead.

"I bribed the Mayor of Covina to approve a flawed structure.

"I kept the now Defunct Hammer and Tails Construction Company afloat through their many mistakes and used my connections to get them to work for Moneybags.

"I signed us up for the game show after our little escape room tour.

"I paid Alan, aka Assn, to steal Lily's weapon and frame her for the death of Adam's family.

"I tipped off the Government Witness protection program something was up across from the Skins Residence.

"The general populace may not have respected me well, but the police and many government agencies were grateful for my work in the Vietnam War.

"Thus, it was not difficult to convince them that we needed to send Assn in to investigate for them as he was the best spy around, and to send anyone else would have led to unnecessary deaths.

"I gave Mr. Lynx Absinthe to get him drunk and planted the hammer and nails card on Mr. Nightingale.

"I knew in his shock of discovering the card he would pull out his weapon to find it.

"A freshly roused Mr. Lynx would see the card and gun on Mr. Nightingale open fire with his own, and his gang would try to cover it up.

"Being a veteran, I got intimate knowledge of The Heavens Demons.

"Who was likely to betray them and who had recorded as come and gone from the gang?

"In connection to Mr. Nightingale, I met Dalton Dredger, who was none too pleased about what had happened to one of his best contract workers.

"I suggested the best way he could get back and them and commit the perfect crime would be to strike where they least expect it.

"So, he sent Carlos Diablo to try and kidnap Hunter for Dalton, who would put him to death for all to see while anonymous to the public, known only as a member of Heavens Demons.

"Naturally, I did not account for Proctavious spying on Bill's friends, but no matter, I took care of him eventually.

"I encouraged Herbert Harbinger XIV to practice his archery near Henry Skin's targets which wound up getting him killed.

"I gave some prescription drugs to Victor Vindicator or Vanguard, whichever surname he prefers to sell them.

"You may wonder what killed Thaddius Yu then and got us out of that one?

"I called the police to report a kidnapping and murder in progress before you arrived to ensure I got out alive.

"The bullet that did him in came from a member of Heaven's Demons who I tipped off a rat and traitor of theirs may have been found.

"You may think it impossible since the weapons were untraceable to a registered user.

"That is because they were custom-built by Thaddius Yu, bought by me, and given to a select few members of Heaven's Demons. I quickly washed away any forensic evidence on the items once used and planted ones not used on the scenes of the crimes with a bullet missing that matched the model gun in all cases where unknown firearms were involved.

"I convinced Benson to get approval from the UP to give us weapons in case anything I did not plan for happened.

"I got us off the hook evidentiarily.

"And lastly, I let the poor person who sold the poison to the electrician take the fall for it all.

"The final phase of my plan was to hack into Benson's Security Systems, set up this game you all became a part of, and get all of you here.

"Once I learned your weaknesses, it was all too easy.

"People let their guard down when you appear dumb most of the time."

"That still does not explain why you went to all this trouble and would admit to this when we would never have found out.

"What was your motive?"

"I am glad you asked.

"As you may not have remembered from when the team went out for dinner at Clops and earlier in my explanation, before joining your investigative team, I was a Veteran of the Vietnam War.

"I was drafted to serve in it against my will.

"I begged, I did not want to kill anyone, but it was that or military prison for insubordination.

"While Assn was not in military prison, the program that employed him while serving sentences for anything he was required to do for them was not much better.

"There was no opportunity to be a government patsy. You rotted away in the most inhumane conditions imaginable and had fewer rights than a regular civilian.

"Considering how much Assn loved the Witness Protection Program and the work he got under them, you can guess it was not a place you wanted to be.

"So, I served my time and did my duty, begrudgingly watching as men, women, and children fired upon our fleet.

"And for what?

"To defend a system that by its nature demands that some must fail and die and others must succeed and become filthy rich at the expense of others.

"We had no business being there.

"And you remember the best part?

"When we got home, we were hailed not as heroes, given no thanks for being forced to risk our lives for our Country.

"No civilians saw us as demons!

"They spat on us!

"Called us murderers!

"And you all wanted to accept these 'Furries' who landed here with superior capabilities to all of us?

"Furries who could easily replace any human with a machine to power the worst aspect of Capitalism.

"Automation!

"I felt outsourcing and globalizing a far lesser evil by comparison since it is still a human doing the job.

"And you know what else?

"Your World War II vets were hailed heroes despite being drafted the same and getting involved in the worst genocide in human history.

"It is just not fair!

"I could understand if we had a choice to go serve, but I remind you.

"Being drafted cost me, my friends, the love of my life, and our kids, and they all left me.

"They left because they did not want to be associated with my service.

"So, you and your Country can take it up your mother fucking asses or tail holes with a twelve-foot pole for all I care!

"Do not be fooled into thinking everything will return to normal even if you catch me.

"It will not.

"You cannot erase the racism I have influenced, the hate, the desire for vengeance, or the mistrust that made this all possible.

"I am not finished with any of the ones you have come to love.

"You think the story is over, but it has just begun."

The transmission ended, and the cage holding us opened along with the last door as we walked through.

"I... am sorry I had no idea..."

Adam looked at me sternly, "Save it, nothing will bring back what is lost, and I moved on.

"The rest of this planet would do well to do the same lest we get more megalomaniacs like him running rampant on this planet."

Despite his words, something told me he would kill at a chance to see that man suffer. While there is little chance of catching him without UP intervention since he has fled the Country and we have no units in Russia, and evermore crimes, have been set in motion. Our work may never be done domestically or otherwise. I also could not help but notice he seemed taller than when I rescued him. Adam was six years old when he moved out of California. Now it is like declaring he let go of the past; he finally became an adult. That or my state of mind was imagining it, given the insanity of what I had just learned.

Additionally, time seems to pass more rapidly as one gets older. The others seemed to have changed similarly, except those who still held grudges. What could it mean?

Besides that, I hope the UP can get clearance to find this guy and bring him to justice. Until then, we will pick up the pieces of what was left behind and do what we must mitigate the damage caused. Speaking of mitigation of injury, I would be remiss not to mention that in light of this new evidence, Lily Lockup used it in Appeals court. She was acquitted because of a mistrial, proving Lily did not do as she was suspected, and she regained custody of her adopted children.

Adam went back to Michigan to pursue higher education. Hard to believe he is all grown up and ready to make a name for himself. Last I heard, he was developing a social media app called "Cat Box." Those were not just words of ambitions he had for himself while we were trapped here. That said, I believe I share Neko's Cynicism that it will do anything to curb the propensity of malicious entities to act as such in the real world. Neko quickly started studying Golf and putting together campaigns to take it to the next level. With investment from intergalactic sources, I soon found them popping up all over the USA in numbers that would make Galactic Cash Coffee blush. With Help from Neko's Business Success Kit Kit and Kit Kat eventually made their TV shows happen. Isaac joined a band with Adam and Neko and toured the Earth and, ultimately, the Galaxy. Adam would also get to enjoy success with his TV and radio shows.

Sadly, in light of the crimes of the human race against furry kind, it seemed unlikely they would be trusted with hover cars anytime soon or anything that would make their lives easier, with some exceptions. They at least helped Africa end world hunger with their infinity plates. Don Giovanni retired in peace, Hunter became a local attraction for Torrance, and Axel Flask joined a traveling renaissance fair and was among the most successful vendors. Sofer continued to publish books and poetry while working various jobs, including as an office assistant for Switch Golf, before eventually reaching enough renown to live off his writings. Carlos Diablo continued to be a contractor while in the witness protection program. Herbert Harbinger XIV finally found his passion for Golf, and his Father approved.

Victor Vindicator finished his prison work program and founded a company for transspecies and gender-nonconforming individuals to find work suitable to their skill set. It was not without help from various other furry organizations that popped up simultaneously to help. Judge Accurate got promoted to "Intergalactic Court Judge" and can now preside over cases involving interplanetary affairs. Not much else happened for the Lawyers he frequently saw as they could be hired the same as any other lawyer and pass the bar to be intergalactic if they chose. Same with some of the other judges. The orphans got psychological help, as did their mother, and saw themselves in suitable jobs. The children who had their college paid for by Herbert Harbinger XIV's Father went on to become doctors and nurses. The Hatfields and Mc Coys partnered up to make an attraction surrounding the actual case in Chapter 2 and were highly successful.

As for my team, Bill Benson was promoted to "UPI Chief" or "United Planets Investigation Chief." My remaining teammates and I all got taken on by the UP as special agents. We could now be sent on hazardous missions to investigate crimes wherever they happened in the Galaxy with some limitations. We could not be shipped to countries that did not sign a pact with them. Russia was off the table unless Earth elected a United Planets Representative from a majority of the citizens of the planet, irrespective of Country. That or passed a Law to make an exception for those of significant threat to our interests. Perhaps in the next book, that will happen, but until then, this is the happiest ending for everyone involved.

ABOUT THE AUTHOR

Adam Thomas Applebaum is the author of 6 books as of this publication. He holds a Bachelor of Science in Business Administration and is concentrated in Information Systems. Adam founded a seasonal popup store that would make convention appearances and operate solely online outside of that in 2016. He has offered both self-published books he wrote, calligraphy, and poetry services. Adam has a YouTube channel related to that side venture. It aired its first video on March 09, 2021, where he reads creepypastas, demonstrates how he writes poetry, and helps us get in touch with emotions men were expected to repress for generations. He also controlled a mostly variety archive channel for things he did on a whim since YouTube began but only uploaded his first video on February 15, 2010.

Adam's most significant influence for his value of being well-read and prolific was his late Great Grandma Frances Zimmer, who died of Alzheimer's. He said, "She knew how to take a board or card game and take me out of the competitive tension of it by conversing about unrelated things." She also gave him a light blue and white glow-in-the-dark teddy bear as a baby, which he regrets selling or donating as a teen, and just this year bought a replica of it in like new condition. The image of said item is on the last page and has since been an easter egg throughout this and other works Adam has created. It does not necessarily mean to the reader that something tragic is about to happen. Those who are said to hold such a specific item will have a much more significant role before them than any reasonable person may expect of them when it is bestowed. It could be anything from being the main character of their own story to someone of interest in a case, as was seen in this book. Though some supposedly own these items, not all of them will have anything extraordinary happen to them. Instead, their being "written" to have it in their possession makes them a person of interest, if at all. Adam grew up in Covina and moved to Torrance at 14, so it should be no coincidence that many exciting things happen in both places. The black and white Maine Coon, some of you saw on the back cover of previous books, Jimmy, died July 05, 2020, of complications from anemia found after a flea bath. Adam has a rock holding the remnants inside, a clay pawprint, and a picture of him as a kitten.

Adam went from being a cashier and quality assurance analyst to an office admin and now lives independently of his parents in an apartment in Los Angeles, California. Since leaving them, he has not stopped writing and probably will not soon. Nevertheless, since the move, Adam has focused more on professional development than attending conventions and meetups. If he could run any brick-and-mortar business in the world, he would want to own a bookstore where people who are not traditionally published could have their works sold. Adam would carry almost exclusively book titles not found in significant book retailers except online, barring his store. Adam might also sell custom poetry as he does online, depending on how many people he expected to visit the store regularly and how many employees he had working with him. Adam does not quite know if he could make this work long-term or secure the necessary funding, but perhaps it will be something he does when he can afford to retire.

What the next installment in this new series will hold, time will tell, but currently, Adam is considering more of a chase mystery for the next novel where we already know who the team is after, but they do not know where exactly they are or when. Other considerations include revisiting other Universes across this greater Multiverse to tie up loose ends and maybe explain how our main protagonist here ended up in the previous series a little less than halfway in. Perhaps it is better not to think too hard about the past and instead press on toward the future.

CONTACT US
Phone: 310-561-6330
Email: theforsakenscribe@gmail.com
Website: www.theforsakenscribe.com

Fan Mail:
Adam T Applebaum

PO Box 14606
Torrance, CA. 90503

Social Media:
Facebook: https://www.facebook.com/TheForsakenScribe
Instagram: @Adathorrules
Steam: Adathorrules
Twitter: @ScribeForsaken
Telegram: https://t.me/TheForsakenScribe & @AdamTheForsaken
Discord: AdamTheForsaken#2081
YouTube: @theforsakenscribe6933 and @AdamApplebaum

My Teddy Bear
Lloyd Bear Company

www.ingramcontent.com/pod-product-compliance
Lightning Source LLC
Chambersburg PA
CBHW030544310726
48979CB00010B/2024/J

* 9 7 8 0 9 9 7 0 5 0 5 3 0 *